Copyright © 2024 by Marci Bolden

All rights reserved.

No part of this book may be reproduced in any form or by any electronic or mechanical means, including information storage and retrieval systems, without written permission from the author, except for the use of brief quotations in a book review.

This is a work of fiction. Names, characters, businesses, places, events, locales, and incidents are either the products of the author's imagination or used in a fictitious manner. Any resemblance to actual persons, living or dead, or actual events is purely coincidental.

Cover design by Amber Maxwell.

ISBN: 978-1-950348-79-4

PRESTIGE

MARCI BOLDEN

PINK SAND
PRESS

PROLOGUE

Personal security guard Troy Buchanan took in the scene at the so-called safe house.

Blood spatter covered nearly every surface of the living room. The couple he and his team had been protecting had clearly been tortured prior to being killed.

Richard Bantam's stomach had been slit open and his innards placed on his chest. *Disemboweled.* The method of choice for killing snitches in the circles Richard had run in for decades. Sharon, his wife, used to talk a mile a minute. Now her tongue was gone, and her throat slit. Their deaths had been violent and painful. Even more—the grisly killings would send a message to anyone else who might be thinking about oversharing with the feds.

Troy and his team were responsible for keeping their clients safe. They didn't always like who their clients were, and that was definitely the case now. Though this client was a financial advisor, Troy was fairly certain Richard had earned his millions by stealing from others—skimming here, overcharging there, hiding money. Before going into hiding, he'd seen Richard with less than stellar people, including runners for Gunner Escobar—the latest head of the Escobar family drug cartel.

As soon as he'd started to put the pieces together, he'd suggested that perhaps the Bantams weren't their ideal clients, but that wasn't his call. The money was good, and apparently that was more important than keeping the Lochlin name clean.

Troy had been with the security firm for almost a decade, and this was the first time one of his clients had been murdered in all those years. Lochlin Private Security did more than simply protect politicians, celebrities, and other elites. The firm hired highly trained guards and investigators to not only protect their clients but dig deep into the shadows to root out those who threatened them. They were the best of the best in the business. People didn't die on their watch.

This was bad. On so many levels.

Richard had hired Lochlin Private Security because he'd started receiving increasing threats, though only Troy's superiors knew exactly what those threats had entailed. Troy was the lead on this team and was supposed to keep the Bantams safe. But soon after he took the case, Troy started to suspect the Bantams were in more danger than he had been told. Troy's gut had told him to keep close to them. Too bad that instinct hadn't been enough to keep them alive.

Just last week, he'd asked that the family be transferred to a safe house where they could be better protected. This was supposed to be a safe place. No one was supposed to know the Bantams were here.

Standing in the blood-stained room made Troy feel sick to his stomach, but not because of the gory crime scene. The only way the Bantams could have been found and murdered was if his gut had been right. Someone with inside information was responsible for this.

Now the Bantams were sprawled across the living room of their new home as blood dried on the walls, the ceiling fan, and soaked into the gray shag carpet.

Not all the Bantams were accounted for, however.

"Where's Logan?" Troy asked.

The six-year-old boy who cried every night because he missed his room, his toys, and his friends was not among the fatalities in the living room.

Sharon had tried to make this like a vacation for her son, but she was scared, terrified of something that no one wanted to share with Troy and his team. Logan had picked up on her fear, and that had fed into his own.

Troy didn't have a kid, but even he knew they should have tried harder to protect Logan.

"We haven't found him," Randall Gillion said. "They probably took him."

Troy didn't blink, didn't jolt, but he did hold his breath for a second.

His colleague came to that conclusion without much emotion. Troy knew being hardened against violence was part of the job, but Randall's lack of compassion for the child was a red flag that Troy tucked away in the back of his mind with the rest of the flags he'd been collecting over the last few weeks—like the gold watch that sparkled on Randall's wrist when he checked the time before making a note on his little pad. He'd been wearing a scratched-up leather band the week before.

When Troy had asked about the new watch, Randall had dismissed it and said it had been a gift. He'd gotten a good enough look to verify the brand name. Omega. How did a guy like Randall receive such an expensive gift as an Omega watch?

Hank Malony, another member of the team, said, "We'll get a group looking for the boy. If he isn't dead, he'll be for sale soon."

Just as Troy's gut had told him the Bantams were in danger, his gut also told him Logan wasn't about to be put on the black market. And Troy always listened to his gut.

Their old team leader had pounded into their heads that they listen to their instincts. She said they didn't have to believe in karma or God or anything else, but they damned well better believe what their guts told them. Troy did. He'd known something bad was going to happen. He'd tried to warn his supervisors. Nobody had listened.

Troy hoped Logan had listened. He hoped the kid heard every word Troy had told him when he'd pulled him aside and showed him where to hide if something went down.

"Any idea who did this?" Troy asked.

Randall scoffed. "I don't think we have to reach too far to know it was the Escobars."

"Not who was responsible," Troy clarified. "Who did the deed."

Hank kneeled beside Sharon's body and grimaced. "Somebody with a strong stomach. This is vile."

"I've seen worse," Randall said and then proceeded to

share details of a rape and dismemberment when he was a cop.

Troy tuned him out. Randall always had a story to outdo everyone around. He'd let him and Hank determine who had seen the worst of the worst.

Slipping away from the team he'd grown suspicious of, Troy moved down the hallway of the contemporary ranch house to Logan's bedroom. The room was decked out in a race-car theme that the little boy had confided in Troy that he hated. Looking around the room, Troy's heart started beating faster.

The red race-car-shaped bed had been flipped over, and the clothes from the closet had been tossed on the floor. Whoever had broken in had looked for the boy. They'd intended to kill him too.

Troy looked down the hallway, verifying he hadn't been followed, before easing the bedroom door shut. Moving to the window, he slid the glass pane open and popped the screen. Poking his head out, he checked that the small grassy area was clear. A week ago, when his suspicions grew into real concern, he'd crept around the back of the house and loosened three boards in the wooden privacy fence. Removing those boards would leave a big enough hole so a grown man and a little boy could escape in a hurry.

Crossing the room in three long strides, Troy aimed his flashlight toward the ceiling of the closet. He whispered the code phrase Logan had chosen: "Race cars suck."

A moment later, Logan peered out from the top of the shelves. His dark-brown eyes were wide, and his lip trembled. Troy pressed his finger to his mouth to signal Logan to be quiet, and then he gestured for the boy to come out of hiding.

Logan climbed down the shelves and, without a word, took Troy's hand. Troy glanced through the window and confirmed the backyard was still empty. Thankfully, the guards were still focused on the bloody scene in the living room. He lifted Logan through the window, then he climbed through the opening too. Once safely on the grass outside in the yard, he pulled the window closed behind them and replaced the screen so they didn't immediately tip off anyone who walked into the bedroom.

Troy guided the boy through the loose boards and then followed him. In the alley, Troy hefted Logan onto his back and hooked his arms around the kid's thin legs. Logan clung to him, hugging tight, as Troy ran off into the night.

[1]

MERI OSBORNE TRIED to hide her irritation as she watched the woman across the table blowing her nose into the third tissue she'd plucked from the box that sat on the Prestige Security and Investigation Services conference room table. Though the conference room was the largest in the modest-sized office setting, the walls were close enough to echo the sniveling and whimpering coming from the woman.

Meri wasn't the most sympathetic member of the team, but she'd done a pretty good job of reassuring and offering condolences to the woman who was convinced her husband was cheating.

More times than not, the person hiring them was right—his or her spouse was cheating. The private investigators were responsible for getting proof, which usually led to more of this type of emotional display either in their office or in divorce court as they testified to what they'd witnessed. Meri, however, wasn't an investigator. She worked security.

Or she had until she'd joined this team. Part of her

skillset as a professional security provider was blending into the background. That was perfect for someone trying to snap photos of a lying, cheating spouse.

After a year of working cases like this, Meri was learning to fake the sympathy their clients needed. The fact that the entire Prestige team was female drew in women like Ana Cortez. They likely assumed they'd find genuine comfort here, but that maternal gene had somehow skipped Meri's DNA. She'd spent too much of her career dealing with liars and scumbags to easily dip into the sensitivity their clients sought.

Some of her other teammates were natural caregivers, but Meri had to bite her tongue so she didn't tell the woman to toughen up and confront the bastard. That'd save her time, heartache, and the money she was about to spend having her husband followed.

As the pile of used tissues in front of Mrs. Cortez grew, Meri's desire to work with this woman decreased. She cast a glance to her left, assessing her team leader's reaction in a split second. Lynn Sanchez sat stoic, as unemotional as a statue as she waited for their potential client to gather herself enough to answer why she was so confident her husband was seeing someone else.

They were used to clients getting emotional while explaining their cases. However, Mrs. Cortez took that to a level Meri didn't think she'd ever seen. The woman had to have been an actress at some point in her life. No one else could possibly display such dramatics with so much ease. The woman was borderline wailing as she explained that she found a receipt for a motel room in her husband's pants pocket.

A knock at the door was a welcome distraction. Trista, the team administrator-slash-Internet sleuth, poked her blond-topped head in. "Excuse me?"

Oh, please need me, Meri silently begged.

"I need you," Trista said, as if she'd read Meri's internal plea.

Meri smiled politely at the crying woman and started to stand.

"Lynn," Trista clarified. "I need Lynn."

Sinking back in her chair, Meri did her best not to let her disappointment show. Returning her focus to the sobbing woman across the table as Lynn rushed toward freedom, Meri picked up her pen again.

"Do you have that receipt with you, Mrs. Cortez?"

As if she were a robot on an assembly line, Meri asked the right questions, gathered the required information, and walked Mrs. Cortez to the door. Before ushering the woman out, Meri assured her that *someone* would be in contact with her soon. She couldn't bring herself to commit to being that person.

Closing the door, she walked straight to her office, not bothering to check in with Lynn to see how she had gotten so lucky as to be pulled from the meeting. As she dropped into the black faux-leather chair behind her desk, Meri tossed her notebook aside with a level of disgust she hadn't intended.

God, she hated working these cases. She spent far too many hours sitting in a car watching people brazenly throw away the lives they'd built. If they were so unhappy, why didn't they walk away? That was what she'd done. When her old life had become too burdensome to bear, she'd washed her hands of it and walked away. She'd left before she could hurt those she'd grown to care about. That was what any reasonable and responsible person should do. Not lie, cheat, and deceive. That was the cowardly way out. Leaving was the right thing.

Wasn't it?

She rarely doubted herself, but lately, she had to admit there was a voice in the back of her mind mocking her past decisions. A year ago, before she'd come to Prestige, she'd been responsible for the death of a teammate—not directly, but Sarah's death had been a chain reaction of events that never should have even started. Everything stopped that day. Everything Meri thought she knew about herself caved in on her. She no longer had confidence in herself or her choices. A security guard can't be filled with self-doubt and survive. And she shouldn't have been leading a team.

She'd resigned, walked away from everything—*everyone*—and started over. She'd never questioned that decision until recently. She'd found a new place with the Prestige team. She fit here. That was the only thing she didn't question. But she had started to question if she'd been too rash in walking away. Maybe she should have stuck things out a bit longer to see where the chips would fall instead of assuming she knew.

The kicker was that now she'd begun to doubt being a private investigator. Was following philandering men around actually filling the void she'd created in her life, or temporarily masking the hole inside her? She wasn't sure anymore.

"Meri," Lynn called. "Everything okay?"

Meri nodded rather than telling a blatant lie.

Lynn noticed. In fact, everyone on her team had noticed she wasn't herself these days. Some had asked why, others hadn't bothered.

She loved that the Prestige team was so supportive of each other, but she tended to keep her problems to herself. Not only because she didn't want to burden others, but she couldn't very well tell them she was questioning everything about her life, including if she really belonged at the agency. Even though she fit here, she was no longer certain she had made the right decision to walk away from her old life.

The day she had resigned, her former boss told her there would always be a place for her at the agency. Whenever she was ready to return, he'd make a place for her. Of course, at that point, he didn't know everything there was to know about Sarah's death. He surely did by now and might have a different opinion of Meri.

The other side of that was that she didn't think she could possibly walk away from her new life. These women had become her family. Her sisters. She felt especially close to Lynn. They had the same dry wit and serious attitude. Too serious sometimes, Meri suspected. Lynn was loosening up, though. She was engaged now, soon to be married, and Meri figured a woman who had someone to go home to made her feel she could relax and enjoy life a bit more.

As she entered Meri's office, Lynn eased the door shut so the click didn't alert any other members of the team. A closed door in their office was like a siren's song, luring others closer to hear office gossip. If any other member of their team got the idea that some great secret was being shared, they'd all be crammed in Meri's office trying to solve her life problems.

Sitting in the chair across from Meri's desk, Lynn held her gaze. "What is it? What's been on your mind lately?"

Meri cocked a brow, her universal and completely effective way of making someone shut up.

"If you say nothing, I'll break your kneecaps," Lynn said.

Meri smiled as she tempted fate. "It's nothing."

The two shared a quiet laugh before returning to their usual serious natures.

"Talk to me," Lynn said.

Unsettled. That was the only way Meri could describe how she'd been feeling. But she couldn't really explain why. When she'd started this new job, she'd been determined to keep herself at arm's length. Getting too close had been her last mistake.

But it hadn't taken long for her to get invested in each and every member of her team. Not only did she want them to succeed, but she *needed* them to be safe—though she knew she couldn't always do that. That sense of failure hit a bit too close to home after burying Sarah.

Lynn tried again. "You have been distracted for weeks. Why?"

Tapping her fingers on her desk, Meri let out a measured breath. "Honestly? I think I'm a bit restless. I've been here a year. I'm settled in."

Concern lit in Lynn's eyes as she read between the lines. "You're unhappy."

"No." She nearly tripped on the word. "I don't know. I feel...restless. Like I said."

"These damn adultery cases." Lynn frowned. "Nobody likes spying on cheating spouses, Meri. But the money—"

"I know. Easy work, quick payment."

"We have basic expenses to cover that can't wait for more in-depth cases to be resolved."

"*I know*," Meri said again.

Lynn was right on both counts: they did need the money, and nobody liked working these cases. She had quickly learned that was the downside of being in the private investigator business. There was never a lack of people willing to step out on their partners, and they were never as clever about it as they thought. Usually, it didn't take more than a few days to catch the cheater in the act. Those regular invoices paid the bills.

Lynn's frown deepened. "If you want something more challenging, we can try expanding into cold cases. We're more established now. I can approach the D.A. and see about helping them more."

"I'm not going to leave, Lynn," Meri stated. That was the one thing she did know. She was filled with nervous energy these days, but she definitely was not planning to leave. "I love it here. I love the team. I'm not leaving."

Lynn didn't readily show emotion, but her smile was clearly one of relief. "Good. We need you. *I* need you. Can you imagine me handling this group of misfits on my own?"

Meri chuckled. The team kept their leader on her toes.

"You know what you need?" Lynn asked. "An afternoon at the range. Go shoot some targets and clear your head."

That sounded great, but Meri needed to get started on

her new case. She was about to say that when Lynn snagged her notebook.

"I'll give this to Marta."

Meri widened her eyes with surprise. "Marta? Since when is she doing surveillance?"

"Since now." Lynn tore the pages from Meri's pad and dropped it back as she stood. "She asked to start doing more than research. I'm open to that. Our client list is steadily growing. We could use another investigator. She's shown some real initiative. I think she's ready. I'll work with her on this. Don't worry about it."

Oh, Meri was going to worry. Not because she didn't trust Marta. The girl was smart as a whip and had learned plenty of self-defense moves if she ever needed them. The women trained together often, practicing various means of protection. Marta had been a natural at learning Casey's Aikido moves. Meri was more worried about the reputation of the company. Prestige was still relatively new, and she didn't want a simple case to inadvertently get blundered.

"I should—"

"She has to start somewhere if she wants to do more than offer up legal advice and keep our licenses and permits up to date. And, like I said, we could use another investigator. She can do both." She gave a resolute nod. "It's fine. You take the afternoon off. We'll get to work on finding more interesting cases for you tomorrow."

Lynn disappeared without another word to reassign Meri's unwanted case.

Guilt tugged at Meri's gut as she looked at the notebook that moments ago had held the information on Ana Cortez's husband. Meri hadn't cared much for the woman, but she hated not following through. Something about Ana didn't sit right with Meri, and she worried Marta might not pick up on that. Of course, she could be passing a harsh judgment on someone who was going through what that woman was. An unfair judgment. One that Marta probably wouldn't make since she was clearly far less bitter than Meri was these days.

Damn. Lynn was right. Meri did need to clear her head.

After gathering her things, she slipped out of the office unnoticed. However, she didn't drive to the shooting range where her team bonded by chiding each other on their marksmanship. She headed home, to the quiet sanctuary of the little one-story house she'd started renting when she'd decided this place was as good as any to replant her roots.

Maybe she should start looking for a place to buy. Casey was house shopping with her boyfriend. At least once a week, the team sat by as she scrolled through images saying things like, "I don't know" and "It's cute, but..." or "The yard is too big. We don't need that much yard."

Meri had seen a few houses that she had loved and couldn't understand why Casey didn't even want to look at them. Maybe it was time Meri looked at them. Perhaps that would ease the nagging in the back of her mind that was making her wonder if she'd walked away from her old life too easily.

Her internal debate raged as she drove to the suburban area she called home. She didn't mind living in the city, but she hated how close the houses were in the newer developments. While Casey didn't want a big yard, Meri thought one of the perks of living in the Midwest would be a big, covered porch looking out over acres of her own land. Not that she'd do anything with that much property. She couldn't keep a houseplant alive, let alone tend to a garden or a farm. But having that much space to call her own would be nice.

Creating a mental wish list of what she'd like in a home kept her occupied as she drove. She definitely wanted at least an acre. A fireplace. A big bathtub. An open concept. She wanted to be able to see her surroundings. And three bedrooms, because she wanted dedicated space for a home office and...

Meri's thoughts halted as she pulled into her driveway. Though she didn't overtly react, she studied the wooden blinds covering her living room window. They were closed. All the way. She never closed them all the way. She left them open enough to let the natural light in while keeping prying eyes from easily seeing inside.

She remained calm, casual, acting as if she hadn't noticed as she gathered her things. Instead of pressing the button on her remote to open the garage door, she parked in the driveway, then opened her car door and climbed out. She scanned the surrounding area so innocently, most people wouldn't have noticed what she was doing. There were a few cars on the street, but she didn't see any sign that they were occupied. Nothing stood out to her or made her feel like she was about to be ambushed.

When she was convinced she wasn't being watched by anyone in the immediate area, she quietly closed her car door. Whoever had turned her blinds may still be inside. She didn't want to alert them that she was home if they hadn't noticed, but she also didn't want to appear alarmed if they had. Letting an intruder think he had the upper hand was the best way to overtake him. Or *her*, since women were as capable of committing crimes.

Normally, Meri would walk to the mailbox at the end of the driveway before going inside, but today, she was hesitant to turn her back on her house. Instead, she walked right for the door, opening her bag as she went. She reached in as if looking for something, but she was actually wrapping her hand around the subcompact Glock 26 she kept inside while simultaneously switching the safety off. If someone was keeping track of her movements, going for the gun on her hip would be too obvious. By acting oblivious, she hoped pulling a weapon from her purse would give her an element of surprise if needed.

At her front door, she gently tested the knob. It didn't turn.

Sliding her key silently into the lock, she turned it as slowly as she could, limiting the telltale click as the bolt disengaged. With her keys still dangling, she dropped her purse, pushed the door open, and lifted the gun in her hand, taking aim at a man standing in her living room.

He already had his hands up as if expecting this scene to play out exactly as it had. The man, with his short-cut brown hair and gray eyes, stood in silent surrender. Recognition eased her tension, and she exhaled the breath she'd been holding as she lowered the gun.

She hadn't seen that face in over a year. He looked worn down, stressed, but she knew he wasn't there to hurt her.

"What the hell are you doing here?" she demanded.

Troy Buchanan dropped his hands once the gun was no longer pointed at him. "We come in peace."

Before she could ask who *we* was, a tiny thing no more than six years old with big, terrified eyes peered around his hip.

Troy leaned against the chipped white linoleum countertop sipping coffee while Logan sat on the couch across the room. The television was on, but the boy wasn't watching cartoons. He was turned, kneeling on the cushions and peering over the back so he could watch Troy and Meri. He had barely taken his gaze off Troy since they'd slipped out of the safe house.

They'd been on the run for thirteen days, nine of which Troy had spent pinpointing the exact location of the only person he could trust. Three more were spent taking the long way to get to her. And the final day was watching her house to make certain Lochlin Private Security hadn't beaten them here.

From where Meri sat on the other side of the island, she offered the little boy a slight smile. That was about the most reassuring act Troy thought he'd ever seen out of his old team leader. She had never been the affectionate type. She'd once told him the only thing that made her nervous was kids. She somehow had come to terms with that anxiety.

She didn't appear upset at the moment. Or angry that he had shown up unannounced with a child in tow. He had been expecting a full-on shitstorm for disrupting her new life before getting her to calm down enough to hear him out. She was irritated, but she hadn't ripped into him like he had expected.

He hoped this change in her demeanor wasn't a sign that she'd softened over the last year. He needed her sharp mind and sharper edge if he was going to get Logan out of this mess alive.

She returned her attention to Troy and whispered, "Did he see what happened to them?"

Setting his coffee down, he blew out a long breath. "I don't think so, but he certainly had to have heard it. Whoever killed them didn't do it quickly or kindly. I asked if he saw anybody in the house, but he said as soon as he heard yelling, he hid."

"Does he know they're..."

He didn't need her to finish her question. "I don't know."

"You haven't asked?"

Troy frowned at her. "I've had a few things going on, Meri. Besides, if he doesn't know what happened, do you really think he needs to deal with that right now?"

She returned his frustrated look but didn't disagree. "He'll have some trauma to work through. Running like this isn't helping."

"Yeah, well, until I know who to trust, this is the best I can do. I don't know who has been compromised at Lochlin Private Security, and until I figure it out, the only thing I do know for certain is that he is safe with me. I'm pretty sure his father was laundering money for a drug cartel—the Escobars—and his mother shared that information with the wrong people."

"I wasn't implying that you'd made the wrong choice," Meri soothed. "I'm worried what this might be doing to him."

"Me too." Leaning on the island, closing the distance between them, he whispered, "If I can keep him alive long enough, I'll find him a world-class shrink."

She smirked but kept the sarcastic remark that he suspected was on the tip of her tongue to herself. As she sipped from her mug again, her eyes demanded answers to questions she hadn't verbalized. At least that much hadn't changed. She could get a dead man to talk if she stared at him long enough.

"Go ahead," Troy said. "Ask."

She cocked one thin brow. "Ask what?"

"How I found you."

"I know how you found me. I trained you to find people like me."

He shook his head. "You trained me to find sneaky criminals and terrified witnesses. Last I checked, you weren't either."

The right side of her mouth tilted in a grin as she focused much too intently on setting her mug down. "I trained you to find people who don't want to be found, Troy. I'm definitely one of those."

He didn't have to ask why she wouldn't want to be found. He knew. On one hand, he didn't blame her. On the other, he was pissed as hell that she'd disappeared without a word to him. He'd deserved a goodbye and an explanation.

Instead of dredging up the past, he said, "I couldn't use the usual channels to find you. As soon as I disappeared with him, the old channels closed. I had to do a lot of good old-fashioned research, Meri *Osborne.*" He emphasized her last name because it wasn't the name she'd used when she was his team leader at Lochlin Private Security. Back then, her last name had been De Luca. "I'm sure your great-grandmother would be thrilled to know you revived her maiden name. Maybe not as much to know that you've cut your family off in an attempt to go into hiding."

"I talk to my mother at least once a week."

"From a disposable, untraceable phone. She doesn't even know where to send you a Christmas card."

"Is that what she told you?"

He stared at her as he wondered if Mrs. De Luca had lied to him. That sweet little Italian woman who made him homemade meatballs more times than he could count. The woman who would lovingly swat his hand away when he tried to taste the cannoli filling before she could squeeze it into the shells she'd fried. The woman who had stared at him with sad eyes as he pressed her to tell him where Meri had gone. She'd told him she didn't know, and she was heartbroken that her daughter had left as she had.

Troy didn't have family in New York. He had lived in Augusta, Maine, when he'd been hired to join Meri's team. She and her mother had taken him in, making him feel at home. He'd trusted Mrs. De Luca, and she'd lied to his face. Damn.

The amused hint of a grin on Meri's lips turned into an outright smile before she took another drink from her cup. "My mother adores you, Troy. But she's *my* mother, and she knew my job could be dangerous. She knew there might come a time when I had to leave, and she couldn't tell anyone—not even *you*—where I'd gone."

"Right," he muttered.

"Look, just because I quit doesn't mean there aren't a lot of pissed-off criminals out there who would love to get their hands on me for protecting my clients from them. I'm not dragging that into my new life. I left all that behind me." She lifted her brows at him. "Well, I tried to, anyway. I didn't want to be found, so I took steps to put the past behind me. I'm not hiding from the law. Just a few people I'd rather didn't come knocking."

He didn't know if she included him in that group. He hoped she didn't. But he wasn't going to ask because if he did, she'd be brutally honest about where he stood with her. While he hadn't come here for a reunion, he didn't want to get shot down either.

"Well," he said, "you should have put a few more steps in there. It didn't take me long to put the pieces together."

She'd likely never admit it, but he suspected she didn't try nearly as hard as she could have to go into hiding. She'd been one of the best security professionals he'd ever known. When she left, she did so in the blink of an eye and without so much as a cookie crumb to follow. However, once he started digging, he started finding those crumbs and was able to track her down with relative ease. She was better than that. She was smarter than that. He had to wonder if part of her wanted to be found.

When she set her mug down again, she met his eyes, and he could have sworn she looked...peaceful. He'd never seen her look so at ease before. The woman he'd known had always been on high alert, hyperaware of everything. Her last name and the relaxed aura about her weren't the only things that had changed.

A year ago, her hair had a golden hue that almost looked dirty blond in the sunshine. More than once, he'd gotten entranced by the way light bounced off the strands. Those highlights were gone now, but somehow the almost-black shade suited her better. Her clipped accent, native to Brooklyn, New York, where she'd grown up, was missing. Her words came slower and more enunciated now. Her voice was as flat and fake as the shade of her hair.

What she couldn't change was the dark shade of her eyes or the oval shape of her face that made so many people think she was gentler than she was. She had the looks of a sweet kitten but the heart of a jaguar. She knew how to use both to her advantage. That was one of the millions of things that he admired about her.

"I get why you left," Troy said. "What I don't get is why you didn't tell me. I deserved to know you were leaving." He didn't mean for the hurt and accusation to come through, but he'd heard it in his tone, and he knew she had too. She didn't miss things like that. That was why she'd been so damn good at her job.

"Because I needed to start over," Meri said. "If I'd told you I was going to leave, you would have tried to stop me. I would have listened to you. I would have let you convince me to stay, which would have been a mistake for everyone. You might not like it, but you know I made the right choice."

Troy let a flat little laugh leave him. Mostly because she

was right. He would have tried to convince her to stay, and things would have gotten even messier between them.

"Why did you relocate to the Midwest? You're an East Coast kinda gal. That's what you always said."

"Why not? This town is big enough to get lost in but small enough not to have to deal with big-city bullsh—" She cut herself off as she glanced at Logan. Then she crossed her arms as she sat back and leveled her eyes at Troy. "You gonna fill me in on this situation, or what?"

"I did."

"Something bad went down, so you ran off with a client's kid without telling anyone?" Once more, she stared him down in the way that could make the most hardened criminals crack. "If you want my help, you tell me what's going on and you tell me *everything*, Troy."

He moved around the counter and dropped onto the stool next to her so he could talk without Logan overhearing. "Soon after Logan started kindergarten, his mom made a few new friends. Friends she liked to brag to a little too much. Threats started rolling in soon after. We put them in a safe house, but it was compromised so we relocated them a few months ago. We pulled Logan from school and did our best to keep his mom under lock and key—or at least keep her mouth shut. Right away, I knew something was off. I couldn't say exactly what, but I felt it. In my gut. You know that feeling."

She nodded but didn't speak.

"I went to higher-ups," Troy continued. "I told them something was going to happen, that we needed to move the family. They didn't believe me. I didn't have evidence to back up my concerns, so I was told there wasn't room in the budget and a bunch of other horse shit excuses. My suspicions were dismissed. I couldn't do anything to get them to a new safe house, so I made a plan for Logan to follow if something happened. I bought a cheap car with cash and a fake name, put a go bag in the trunk, and parked it near the safe house. Once we got far enough out of town, I ditched the car and we hunkered down until I found you, because, honestly, I don't know who else I can trust. I have no doubt the Escobar family got to someone on the team, but I don't know who. At least not yet."

"Have you contacted anyone since you left? I'm pretty sure they wouldn't dismiss your suspicions now."

He had to swallow hard before admitting a bitter truth. "There's a mole in Lochlin Private Security. I don't know who or how high up he could be."

"Could be a she," Meri countered. "Women are as capable of being sellouts. Don't be so sexist." Her teasing smile broke what remained of the tension between them.

Damn it, he'd missed her. Her face softened, and he realized she'd likely read his mind. She'd had that power since the day they met. That was why they had made such a good team.

She looked away, but he didn't. He'd spent years not being able to admire her like he'd wanted. He'd spent countless nights eating dinner with her or visiting her mother for Sunday dinners. Every time he had to pretend like those were two friends hanging out instead of precious stolen moments that he tucked away to replay in his mind later.

There were no workplace protocols to stop him from

taking in her profile now. He would have been content to stare at her forever, but she caught him. Instead of telling him to quit gawking at her, as he was so openly doing, she pushed herself up and walked into her kitchen. The island stood between them once more, but that wasn't enough to break the connection he'd always felt between them.

"If you can find me," she said, "so can the higher-ups at Lochlin. They're probably already watching this place."

"They aren't," he said confidently. "I wouldn't be here if they were."

"Well, they will be soon enough, then. So what's your plan? And you damn well better have one after showing up like this."

Troy didn't want to admit that this was as far ahead as he'd thought. He'd been in survival mode twenty-four-seven since leaving, and he was exhausted—mentally and physically. He hadn't had enough time to think about who the mole could be or what to do about it. He'd had two missions: protect Logan and find Meri. His brain couldn't process anything beyond that.

"The only plan I have right now is to get a good night's sleep. I haven't had one in weeks. Would you mind playing lookout so I can rest?"

"Of course not. You look like hell. But you need to tell me what you're thinking first."

"I'm about to pass out on my feet, Meri."

She pressed her lips together and leveled that death glare at him.

Dragging a hand over his face, he exhaled a long weary breath. He understood her need to get all the details, but he doubted she understood how bone-deep his exhaustion had run.

"Get the bad guy. Save the kid. Settle down with a nice girl."

"You wouldn't know what to do with a nice girl, Troy. What's your plan? You *have* to have a plan," she pressed.

"I don't," he finally admitted. "Our contingency plans always included counting on our teammates. I can't do that. So...I don't know. I've spent the last two weeks on the run with a kid because I don't know where to turn or who to trust. I don't know what the hell I'm going to do. I know *someone* is going to end up"—he let the silence fill in the acknowledgment that Logan would be dead if Troy handed him over to the agency—"if I don't do everything I can to protect him."

The way her frown deepened let Troy know that was not an acceptable outcome to her. She pushed herself up from where she'd leaned against the counter.

"Hey, Logan," she said as she directed her attention across the room, "you hungry?"

Troy looked back, catching Logan's gaze. Troy probably pounded the don't-talk-to-strangers lecture a bit too hard.

"It's okay. You can talk to her. She's our friend."

Finally, Logan nodded.

"I hear kids like mac and cheese," Meri said. "Is that true?"

He nodded again, this time with less fear shining through his big brown eyes.

"That's good," she said. "That's about all I know how to cook."

Troy knew that was a lie, but it got a small grin from Logan, which he assumed was her goal.

"Go sit with him," she told Troy. "Rest your eyes for a few. I'm on this."

He didn't argue. He was too damn tired to do that. His bones protested as he stood, but the moment he sank into her sofa, they turned to jelly. He practically melted into the cushions. As had been the case for the last two weeks, as soon as he got settled, Logan curled against his side. He ruffled the boy's light-brown curls and let out another long breath.

Troy didn't mean to yawn but couldn't quite help himself. This was the first moment in weeks that he didn't feel like he had to be on high alert. Meri was there to help shoulder that burden. She had peered out the blinds as often as he had since she'd arrived home. Though he thought she seemed far more relaxed than he remembered, she still was on her game enough to keep lookout.

She was going to protect Logan as much as Troy would. That was why he'd hunted her down and broken into her house. Well, that wasn't the *only* reason, but that was the priority. Keeping Logan safe was all that mattered for now. He'd settle his other issues with Meri later.

[2]

MERI JOLTED when her head rolled forward. She couldn't remember the last time she had all but fallen asleep on her feet, but she'd dozed off standing guard in her living room. Stretching, hoping to get some life into her muscles, she decided she had to give in. Coffee could only do so much to keep her alert.

She had hoped to let Troy sleep a few more hours, but she wouldn't do him any good if she was too tired to react to a situation. She'd been up for nearly twenty-four hours now. Her body and her mind weren't used to this anymore and that could impede her ability to protect Troy and Logan if she had to respond quickly.

Moving silently through the house, she tapped five times on the bedroom door. Funny how she had left her old life, but the habits resurfaced without a single thought or hesitation. Five taps. That was their signal. The knock had said a million different things, but they always were able to decipher the secret meaning.

She pushed the door open as Troy lifted his head off her pillow. She didn't have to tell him she was too worn out to be any good. They had worked together long enough to read the other without either having to say a word. If there had been any other reason than her mind-numbing exhaustion to wake him, she would have barged in barking orders.

Meri stopped in her tracks, and her heart did a funny little flip as Troy eased a tiny bundle from his chest. Logan moaned and tried to cling to him, but Troy responded with a gentle shushing and a few pats on the boy's back, putting him right back to sleep.

A flash of a memory played through her mind. One night, not even two years ago, she and Troy had sat in their favorite restaurant in Koreatown sharing steamed dumplings as they waited for their main courses. He casually asked her if she ever planned on having a family. Though his tone had sounded off the cuff, the way he averted his gaze, focusing on his chopsticks implied his question wasn't asked in the spur of the moment. That was something he'd been wondering for some time and had found the right moment to ask.

She hadn't hesitated before shaking her head and firmly telling him she had no intentions of bringing children into this dangerous mixed-up world. Her answer had caused the light in his eyes to dim a little. He'd been disappointed. He hadn't said as much—he never would have—but she could read him like an open book.

That wasn't the first inkling she'd had that he was interested in her. Nor was it the first attempt she'd made at being harder and colder than she really was in hopes of pushing him back a few steps.

Of course she'd thought about having a family and settling down. She'd seen some pretty ugly things in her life that gave her pause, but if she'd met the right man...

She couldn't have told him that. That would have been like dumping black powder on the fire smoldering between them.

He'd slipped his mask of a smile back into place and said he planned to have an entire bushel of kids. She then told him she didn't think kids came in bushels. They'd shared an awkward laugh before moving on to a different subject.

The memory faded as he sat up, causing the bed frame to squeak. He ran his hands over his hair, and another memory sparked. She pushed that one away before it even had a chance to replay in her mind.

After clearing her throat, Meri whispered, "Sorry. It's been a long time since I pulled an all-nighter. I'm tapped out. I know you're tired too, but I need to rest for a few minutes, then we can swap again."

"It's okay," Troy said with a gravelly voice. He opened the nightstand drawer and pulled out his gun and the clip. "This is the most sleep I've gotten in weeks. Is there coffee?" he asked as he stood and put his gun in the holster resting on his hip.

"Yeah. A fresh pot."

"Thanks." He stretched, and Meri focused her attention on the bed. "Should I sleep in the chair? I don't want to scare him."

"No. It's fine. He likes you."

As Troy neared the open door, the dim light highlighted the lazy smile that toyed with his thin lips and caused that hint of a dimple in his right cheek to deepen. His light eyes, though he'd just woken up, were more alert than they'd been a few hours ago. He didn't appear as burdened by his situation.

She never had allowed herself to admit to him how much she'd missed him, but she couldn't ignore how having him back in her space felt right. Some might say the circumstances could be better, but these were the circumstances that she and Troy had always found themselves in. This was their job. Protecting someone. This was their world, and being back in it took the edge off the uneasiness she'd been feeling lately.

Whatever Logan's parents had done, the little guy didn't deserve the terror he must be feeling now. That tuned into the side of Meri that her team referred to as her mama bear. Which she found amusing since she wasn't a mama and suspected she never would be. But she understood what they meant. She barely knew the kid crashed out in her bed, but she would burn the world down around her before she'd let some monster harm him. She couldn't imagine how protective real mothers must feel.

"I like him too," she admitted. "He said my mac and cheese is way better than yours."

Troy laughed quietly. "He's a smart kid."

"I need an hour or so to recharge," she said as he stepped around her. "Then you can get some more rest if you need."

"Thanks. I have to start thinking about our next step. Maybe we can hash that out when you wake up."

She watched him leave, easing the door closed as quietly as she'd opened it. She slipped her shoes off and pulled her gun from the holster on her hip. After removing the clip, she put it and her gun in the drawer and put her cell phone on the wireless charger that was a permanent fixture on her nightstand.

As soon as she eased back on the mattress, her body thanked her for the reprieve. She'd been awake for far too long and was definitely feeling it.

She would have immediately fallen asleep if it weren't for Logan rolling into her. He curled into her side, like he had been balled up against Troy's. Even in his sleep, the poor kid was desperate to feel safe. She pulled the blanket up, covering him to his chin. She wasn't much of the maternal type, but she knew to do that much.

One more deep breath, and sleep lulled her under. She didn't stay that way long, though. A shrill ping from her cell phone filled her ears, causing her to nearly jump to her feet.

Logan gave a whimper, also startled by the sound. He grabbed on to her as she reached for her phone. His little fingers squeezed as he panted.

"It's okay," she whispered. "It's my alarm." She swiped the touchscreen to end the sound and dropped back onto the bed, focusing on leveling out her breathing. "Come here," she said and pulled Logan against her side. "I'm sorry, kiddo. I forgot to turn it off." No way in hell she was getting up for her five-a.m. workout routine today. However, she suspected that Lynn would be up soon if she wasn't already.

As she held Logan against her with one hand, she used her other to tap out a text letting her boss know she would be in late and suggesting the team meeting go on without her.

She figured the cryptic text would cause Lynn more

concern than she already seemed to have, but Meri would have to deal with that when she got to the office. Right now, all she could think about was how much she hated sleeping on edge. That was almost as bad as no sleep at all, and a long time had gone by since she'd had to get by on semi-sleep. Her brain was far too foggy.

"Where's Troy?" Logan asked, clearing what was left of the cobwebs in Meri's mind.

"He got up so I could take a nap. He's in the other room."

"Can I go?"

She frowned, not because of his question or even his desire to be with the man who had been his sole protector for the last two weeks, but because that meant she had to get out of bed first, and her bones were still aching from exhaustion.

"Let me go check. Stay put until I say so."

"I know," he whispered. "Troy has the same rules."

Every muscle in her body protested as she rolled to sit on the edge of her bed. She tilted her head, listening intently for any odd sounds coming from the other room. When the house remained silent, she slid her drawer open and collected her weapon. After tucking her phone in her pocket, just in case, she eased her way toward the window. She moved the blinds enough to peer out. All seemed well on the street. When she looked out the other window that faced her neighbor's house, nothing looked out of the ordinary there either.

Next, she moved to the bedroom door and held her breath as she listened. The other side was quiet. One glance over her shoulder confirmed Logan had stayed put, like she'd told him. She pressed her finger to her lips anyway—a warning to be quiet—then slowly opened the door.

She'd moved to the entrance of the living room when she spied Troy at the front window, peeking outside as she had done. He looked back and immediately met her gaze.

"Clear?" she asked.

"Clear."

"Logan's up. Can I send him in?"

Troy nodded. "Yeah."

She didn't have a chance to relay the message. Logan darted around her and straight to Troy, who hugged him tight before ruffling his light-brown hair. The scene pulled at something unfamiliar to Meri, and she had to look away.

The coffee pot still had more than enough for her to have a cup, so she focused on fixing herself a drink while Troy talked to Logan about the options he'd found for breakfast. Which wasn't much, Meri knew. She usually went to the office right after her morning workout and shower. There were always bagels or something in the break room to hold her over until lunch.

"There's a twenty-four-hour store a few blocks from here," she offered as she stirred sugar into her drink. "I can run and get some cereal or something."

"Can we have pancakes?" Logan whispered.

Though he was asking Troy, Meri piped up. "Yeah. I make mean microwave pancakes. What kind of juice do you want?"

Disappointment filled Logan's eyes as he looked up at Troy. "Can we have *fresh* pancakes? I haven't had fresh pancakes since—"

Troy silenced him with a hand on his head, but he was looking at Meri. "Tell you what. You run to the store and buy the mix, and I'll make pancakes."

"Yes," Logan hissed.

Ah. She saw how this was going to be. Two against one. She would be offended if they weren't so adorable now that they'd gotten some rest.

"Fine," she said, lifting her hands in a show of surrender. "Let me hop into the shower real quick so I can finish waking up. You two make a grocery list. A *short* grocery list. I don't need a bunch of food nobody's going to eat."

"I'll eat it," Logan said. "I'm a good eater."

She carried her mug with her to the bathroom as her guests worked on making a list for breakfast. She heard a mention of bacon and had to chuckle. They'd likely eaten nothing but fast food the last two weeks. No wonder Logan was acting like Troy agreeing to make pancakes from a mix was the best thing he'd ever heard.

Meri grabbed a fresh set of clothes and went right to her bathroom. As the water in the shower heated up, she took a sip of coffee and examined the dark circles under her eyes.

She couldn't blame that on lack of sleep. She'd been looking drained for a while now. Strange how even though she was exhausted, she felt more herself this morning than she had for a long time. She'd stood on her feet half the night and only got a few hours of shut-eye but somehow felt better than she had for as long as she could remember.

Instead of reading too much into what that might mean, she set her cup aside and tested the temperature of the water. Satisfied with the heat level, she went to work on undressing.

She only managed to untuck her blouse and release the first button before the bathroom door was thrown open.

Meri instinctively grabbed for the gun on her hip, until she noticed Troy shoving Logan toward her so quickly, the little boy's legs could barely keep up the pace.

"Someone's here," Troy said with a panic-laced voice.

Before Meri could respond, tell him that he should stay while she investigated, he pulled the door closed behind him. She would have followed him, but Logan buried his face in Meri's stomach and whimpered. She looked down at the wavy hair that Troy was so fond of ruffling.

"It's okay," she whispered, pressing her hand to his head. She reached into the shower and turned off the water, then tugged at Logan's arm. "Get behind me. Arms around my waist. Stay right behind me. When I move, you move. Got it?"

He nodded, sniffled, and slid around her. She put one hand on his arms, making sure she knew exactly where he was. As she aimed her weapon at the bathroom door with the other hand, she braced herself for whatever hell was about to be unleashed.

This was far from the first time Troy had found himself in danger, but the way his heart was pounding made staying calm and focused nearly impossible. He knew why. He'd come to care for Logan. The kid was as innocent and sweet as anyone could ask for, and his parents had put him through hell.

And Meri. He'd take a hundred bullets before he'd let her take one. Though he doubted she'd appreciate that. She preferred to be on the front line, but he hadn't given her a chance. He'd left her there with a terrified child she barely knew. He did so with confidence, though. She might not care about Logan in the same way Troy did, but she'd protect that little boy with her life. Just as Troy was prepared to protect them both. He'd die before he let someone get close to that bathroom.

He peered out the front window. The black sedan was still parked on the street, but the woman he'd seen exit the vehicle was nowhere to be seen. She was a professional. He had no doubt about that. The confidence in her stride, the suit she'd been wearing, the way she casually glanced around to assess the area. Everything about her screamed that she was well trained. And deadly.

"Shit," he whispered. He looked to the right, to the left, then at the car again, hoping to see her leaving. She was nowhere to be seen. His panic doubled as he turned to run to the door that led to the attached garage. He'd memorized every window and door in Meri's home long before he'd broken in to ask for her help. He knew there were two windows on the north side of the garage that he could peek through to see if the woman was nosing around the back of the house.

When he spun on his heels, he came face to face with a ferocious-looking blonde who had her handgun aimed at him and a conviction in her eyes that let him know she wouldn't hesitate to kill him. Troy lifted his gun as well. She wasn't the only one who wouldn't have a second thought about pulling the trigger.

They were in a locked-and-loaded stalemate. His vision became laser-focused, and he tuned out everything but her, waiting for the smallest indication that she was going to shoot. He'd shoot too. They'd both go down.

"Who the fuck are you?" she asked in a stone-cold voice.

Troy's lip twitched. "Your worst fucking nightmare."

"Doubtful. You're too cute for that." Though her words mocked him, her tone was hard. "Drop your gun."

"Kiss my ass."

"Well, you're not *that* cute," she said. "Where's Meri?"

Troy calculated the lethal woman's words and tried to decipher the tone she'd used. The initial threat he read off her shifted as he processed her question. She'd asked, *Where's Meri?* Not, *Where's the kid?* She wasn't there for Logan.

"Where is Meri?" she asked more fiercely, lifting her gun a fraction higher.

Troy hadn't had time to delve into Meri's new job, but he did know she was working with a group of female private security officers and investigators. This must be one of them. As far as he knew, no one else would have a reason to break into her house looking for her.

He relaxed his stance, but he didn't take his gun off the woman. The change in his defensive posture was a subtle show that he was willing to talk this out instead of getting into a shooting match.

"I'm a friend of hers," Troy explained. "I needed a place

to crash last night. She's taking a shower right now. She's fine."

The woman tilted her head. "I don't hear the water running."

"Maybe she turned it off." He suspected she had after the way he had stormed in. She would have wanted to hear whatever was happening, and she couldn't have done that with the shower drowning out the sounds.

"Meri!" Silence filled the house as they both listened. "Meri!"

A moment later, Meri appeared in the hallway. "I should have known it was you showing up unannounced," she said flatly. "It's not even six o'clock, Lynn."

The woman still didn't lower her gun or take her eyes off Troy. "You okay?"

"Yeah. I'm fine. Lower the weapon. *Lynn*," she stated more firmly, "lower your weapon."

Finally, the Lynn woman aimed the muzzle of her gun toward the floor, but she didn't holster the weapon or put the safety on. She was ready to fire if needed. Though her distrust of Troy was clearly written on her face, her suspicions made him respect her. She'd walked into an unknown situation with no backup to check on Meri. He would have done the same thing.

"What are you doing here so damn early?" Meri asked.

Lynn finally broke her intense and accusatory stare to look at Meri. "I was worried when you said you were coming in late."

"So you break into my house?"

Lynn looked at Meri as if sending subliminal messages to her. "Your car is in the driveway."

She didn't have to say more than that for Troy to understand what she was saying. Subtle signals were the secret language of security professionals. Apparently, whoever this woman was, she was trained in that area as well. Meri never parked in the driveway. Troy knew that from watching her house the last few days. Lynn must have assumed that was some kind of signal that there was trouble.

"Were you a cop?" Troy asked before thinking.

Lynn looked at him as if he had no right to speak to her before turning her attention back to Meri. "What's going on?"

"I told you in my text. I have things to take care of today."

"Why are you wearing yesterday's clothes?"

Meri pressed her lips together before finally muttering, "Are you serious right now?"

"Yes."

Troy didn't know Lynn, but even he could tell she was serious. He understood why. Many home invasions went unnoticed because the victim acted in compliance, thinking it was the safest way to get through.

Troy stood there with a gun in his hand. Meri could easily be doing her best to get her friend to leave to spare her harm. Situations like this could go a thousand different ways, and it was obvious all three of them were trained well enough to know that.

Clearly, Lynn was being diligent in checking for signs that Meri was in trouble. Meri didn't seem to appreciate the effort, but Troy did. He was glad to know that someone had been looking after Meri. She sure as hell wasn't the best at taking care of herself. She never had been.

"My friend spent the night," Meri snapped. "We stayed up late rehashing old times. We both fell asleep. Fully clothed since you're so damned curious."

"How do you know him?"

"We grew up together." She was lying, and he suspected Lynn saw through that. The first day they met was when he'd been assigned to her team at Lochlin Private Security.

"Where?" Lynn asked.

"Brooklyn, Lynn. I'm fine. *Jesus*. I was too tired to get up this morning, so I took a little time off. I was about to get into the shower when you showed up and pulled a gun on him."

Lynn stared, obviously processing Meri's story before shaking her head. "You're lying to me."

"Lynn—"

The muscles in Lynn's jaw bulged as she narrowed her eyes ever so slightly. "If you can't be honest with me about what is going on here, then we have a real problem. And I don't mean some stranger standing in your living room, Meri. We can't be a team if we start lying to each other."

Troy didn't know if Lynn understood the power of the arrow she'd shot at Meri, but he did. Trust was everything in a team. Lies shattered trust. And when that trust was broken, the team crumbled.

And people died.

Sarah had died because the trust had been broken. Meri blamed herself for that, but Troy didn't hold her responsible. He would have told her that if she hadn't disappeared without a goddamned word. Now she was standing there undoubtedly rehashing every mistake she thought she'd made.

She visibly winced as if she'd been stabbed through the heart. The hurt in her eyes was obvious to Troy. Whether Lynn had intended to or not, she'd hit the target. Seeing Meri wounded cut at his gut. He would have gone to her, wrapped a supportive arm around her shoulder, but that would have raised more questions from Lynn. And probably a punch from Meri.

"I showed up unexpected yesterday," Troy offered to try to ease the tension between the women. "Meri didn't know I was in town. I wanted to surprise her." He hoped his explanation would smooth things over between them, but the stare-down continued.

Right up until a scared little voice called out, "Meri?"

Confusion filled Lynn's eyes as a moment later, thin arms slithered around Meri's waist. Troy was mesmerized by the way she naturally put her hand to Logan's little head and reassured him. Meri was the only other person Troy had ever seen Logan cling to like that. He hadn't even sought out that kind of reassurance from his parents. He'd been intimidated by the constant fighting between them, each blaming the other for their situation, and each equally oblivious to how their actions impacted their son.

Troy had noticed the way the boy constantly withdrew into himself and made it a point to connect with him. That connection had saved Logan's life. If Troy hadn't built that trust between them, Logan likely wouldn't have listened when they discussed their secret plan. And he probably would have ended up on that bloody shag carpet with his parents.

Seeing him trust in Meri added to Troy's conviction that coming to her had been the right thing.

"It's okay, buddy," Meri said. She gestured across the room with one hand while the other held Logan close to her. "This is my friend. She stopped by to check on me because I didn't go to work today. She was worried that I might be sick or hurt, that's all. But now that she knows that I'm okay, she's going to go."

Logan might have heard her reassuring him, but Troy—and undoubtedly Lynn—heard Meri kicking the unexpected guest out of her house.

Lynn let out a loud breath. Yeah, she'd heard the message Meri had sent. Instead of leaving, though, she offered Logan a smile—the same kind smile that Meri had given him several times the day before.

"Hi. I'm Lynn. What's your name?"

Lynn was smart. She'd caught on that something wasn't right. The curiosity in her eyes was dangerous and made Troy uneasy. She was seeing through the lies they'd told, lies anyone else would believe, and was trying to get answers out of the kid.

Instead of answering Lynn, Logan hugged Meri tighter.

"I'll call you later," Meri said, dismissing her.

Lynn remained focused on Logan. Getting kids to give up information they didn't know was valuable was much easier than prying it out of adults. Troy would be pissed if he hadn't used that same tactic in the past himself. However, Lynn was underestimating the little guy. Troy had taught him better than to answer questions from strangers. Logan wouldn't speak to anyone unless Troy gave him permission to do so because he couldn't risk him innocently saying the wrong thing.

"Later, Lynn," Meri said more sternly.

"It was nice to meet you and"—she looked at Troy—"your dad."

Logan burrowed even deeper into Meri's stomach. Strangers made him nervous. He might have warmed up to Meri quickly, but Troy knew it was only because he'd been told it was okay to do so. Lynn wasn't going to get anything out of him, so all she was doing was making him even more scared.

Troy was on the verge of telling her to stop talking to his kid. Because in every way that mattered, Logan was *his* kid right now. He didn't have to, though.

Lynn backed down on her own and returned her piercing gaze to Meri. "I'll be looking forward to your call."

The tension between Meri and her was on the verge of eruption, mostly from Lynn. Meri was unnerved by Lynn's confrontation—something Troy never thought he'd see—but not in a way that concerned him.

Meri was clearly upset that Lynn was angry with her, but not scared or intimidated enough to break.

Lynn started for the garage door, then stopped and said, "I busted a window in your garage breaking in to rescue you. Have someone replace it and send me the bill." Then she was gone the way she'd come, through the garage.

The stress didn't leave with her. Meri was upset, and her eyes looked pained.

"Who the hell was that?" Troy asked as he rushed across the room to snag Logan from Meri. Lifting the boy up, he sat him on the barstool where he'd been perched when Troy's quick scan of the street turned into a panicked rush to get Logan to safety.

"My boss," Meri said. "She's smart. She knows this was bullshi—" She blew out her breath as she looked at Logan, then she offered him that somewhat reassuring smile of hers. "She's a very nice lady, Logan. She won't hurt you or Troy. She didn't understand why you were here."

Logan didn't look like he believed her.

Troy wanted to reassure him, but he was feeling a little uncertain himself. "She's going to ask questions."

Meri nodded. "Yeah. A lot of them." She rolled her shoulders, clearly trying to lessen the stress she tended to keep there. "We gotta come up with a plan, Troy. A real one. Because that was only the beginning of Lynn pressing for answers."

He frowned, suddenly recalling the lack of trust in Lynn's eyes and how it has so clearly stung Meri. "Are you okay?"

"I'm fine. But I know her. She's not done yet. We gotta figure out the next step and take it fast."

For the first time, defeat tugged at the back of Troy's mind. Not the kind of defeat that made him think he'd give up or that he wouldn't be able to keep Logan alive. The kind that came with being so damn worn down that he couldn't think. "She snuck up on me, Meri," he admitted. "She got behind me with her weapon drawn before I knew she was there."

"Don't beat yourself up," Meri said. "She's damn good at what she does."

"I should have known she was there." He dragged his hands over his hair. "Two weeks on the run. I'm losing my edge."

"You need rest." She tucked her hair behind her ear as she scanned her living room. He knew she wasn't seeing the plush sofa or the television attached to the wall like a cherished oil painting. She was thinking, contemplating what came next. "You can't do this alone, and it's only a matter of time before someone from Lochlin comes here looking for you. You can't stay here."

Troy laughed flatly. "If you've got an idea, spit it out. I'm all ears."

"We're hitting the road. We have to disappear. And we need to go now before anyone else shows up unexpectedly."

He hadn't realized how much he was hoping she'd come to that conclusion until she had. Until the words were out of her mouth, he expected to crash at her place for a few days before he and Logan were rested and had another plan and had to walk away from her. He hadn't expected her to join him in hiding Logan, but hearing her offer immediately eased his burden.

"What about your job?"

She shrugged. "Lynn will understand. Or she won't. I'm not sending you back out there on your own. Between the two of us, we can figure this out and keep him safe. But we can't do that here, and we don't have time to work it all out right now. Once we're out of here, we will both be able to think more clearly."

"I don't want to keep running," Logan said quietly.

Troy took two long steps and leaned enough so that he and Logan were eye to eye. "I know. Me neither, buddy. I'm really tired too, but that's the smartest thing to do right now." Standing upright, he lifted Logan off the chair and gave him a gentle push. "Brush your teeth and get dressed."

There was the slightest stomping to the little boy's feet, but Troy didn't correct his behavior. Logan was exhausted and had every right to act a little bratty about the hell he was being put through. Troy thought he wouldn't mind stamping his feet and cursing a bit himself.

"Let's get out of here in fifteen," Meri said.

Troy grabbed her arm when she started for the hallway Logan had tromped down. "Thank you. I knew I could count on you."

She gave him a soft smile. "Fifteen minutes, Troy."

"Fifteen minutes," he repeated as she pulled from him.

[3]

With Troy and Logan hiding under a blanket in her back seat, Meri navigated out of her neighborhood. She had no idea where she was going, but that was the plan—or as much of one as she had so far. If she didn't know, nobody could find them. And by nobody, she meant the people after Logan, anyone at Lochlin, or a member of Prestige.

She hated leaving like this. She hated that Lynn was upset with her, but sometimes clients—even if they weren't paying ones—came first. Right now, Meri had to treat Troy and Logan like her clients. She had to go above and beyond to protect them. If that meant begrudgingly leaving a life that she'd told Lynn made her feel restless, then that was what she had to do.

She'd come back once she got Troy and Logan safe. She'd explain to her team that she hadn't meant to lie or deceive them, but she had to put the safety of an endangered child first. They would understand that. How could they resent her for making that choice?

Meri turned left. If she followed that particular street long enough, she'd be nearing the edge of town. Taking a few lesser traveled roads seemed like a good idea. She'd pick up the highway after she was certain they weren't being followed, which at the moment, she was beginning to doubt.

A suspiciously familiar black sedan stayed a few cars behind Meri. When Meri turned right, headed nowhere in particular, the car followed. She turned left, and the car followed again. She heaved a sigh—long and dramatic and filled with frustration. Using the button on her steering wheel, she connected to her wireless system.

"Call Lynn," she said when the voice recognition beeped to let her know it was waiting for her command. A moment later, the ringing of a phone filtered from the speakers.

"Hey," Lynn answered.

Meri didn't return the curt greeting. Instead, she got straight to the point of why she was calling. "What are you doing?"

"Hanging out. What are you doing?"

Shaking her head, Meri ended the call without answering Lynn's question and turned into a big grocery store parking lot. She stopped far from where the other cars had parked.

"Stay under the blanket," she ordered as she waited for Lynn to pull up next to her.

She left the car running and the air blowing so Troy and Logan stayed comfortable while she confronted her boss. She had no doubt the air under the blanket was getting stuffy by now, turning off the air would increase that tenfold in a matter of minutes. However, the blanket was necessary to prevent anyone from noticing Troy and Logan lying across the back seat.

Climbing from the driver's seat, she closed the door and leaned against it, arms crossed as Lynn parked next to her. Lynn got out of her car too. She walked around to her passenger side and leaned against the door, like Meri had done. Other than in her kitchen this morning, Meri couldn't think of a time when there'd been so much palpable anger between Lynn and her. They had clicked the moment they'd met and had been friends since, rarely disagreeing and never with so much vehemence. She hated feeling this kind of strain between them. She'd always appreciated the ease with which they had worked together.

"Where are you headed?" Lynn asked.

"You are one seriously nosy bitch today," Meri accused.

"I'm a private investigator, Meri. I'm a seriously nosy bitch every day."

Meri actually smiled. "True enough." Scanning the parking lot, she drew a slow breath. "This isn't my thing to tell."

"So ask your friend to crawl out of the back seat and tell me."

She wasn't surprised that Lynn had figured out she had passengers. As careful as Meri had been, Lynn had likely been keeping an eye on her house. She probably watched her drive her car into the garage, and right back out a few minutes later. Lynn would have to have been an idiot to have not realized she'd done that to load Troy and Logan into the back seat.

"This is more important than your hurt feelings," Meri said.

Lynn lifted her brows over the rims of her sunglasses. "My hurt feelings? Is there a reason my feelings should be hurt, Meri?"

"You're mad because I'm respecting my client's confidentiality."

"He's not a client."

"How do you know?"

Lynn pressed her lips together, and the air between them grew even more tense. Her nostrils flared as she forced her breath out, and a flush tinted her cheeks. Her anger was on the verge of erupting.

"You said he was a friend. From Brooklyn, remember?"

"He's both."

"Oh, so you're freelancing now?"

Meri shrugged in an attempt to be casual about the situation. "There's no company rule that says I can't."

Lynn scanned the parking lot as Meri had done, but Meri knew she wasn't looking for danger. She was taking a moment to assess Meri's comment and check herself before responding. When she looked at Meri again, the frustration had eased. When she spoke, the anger had been replaced by concern. "And who has your back while you're freelancing, Meri? Because right now, it looks like you're trying to transport your client without anyone keeping track of you. If something goes down, you're on your own. You, more than anybody else, know how dangerous that can be."

"Screw you," Meri spat without thinking. She'd told

Lynn about Sarah's death to explain why she'd left, not so Lynn could use it against her.

"*Screw you,*" Lynn volleyed back to her. "You've spent the last year pounding into everyone's head how we're a team. How nobody does anything without confiding in at least one of us. How nobody goes *anywhere* without telling someone else on the team. How we have to always have someone watching our backs. That only applies to everyone else, huh? You're too tough to need anyone else. Is that it?"

Meri didn't answer. She didn't have a logical response for what she was doing. Because Lynn was right. Leaving without telling her team, hitting the road without backup, was asking for trouble.

"I am worried about you." Lynn yanked her glasses off so she could stare into Meri's eyes, a move obviously intended to hit her point home. "I am worried *for* you. I don't care who that guy is. I don't care what he's done or why he's running. I care about *you*. My teammate. My friend who is smarter than this."

Meri wanted to scream. This very conversation was why she had been hesitant to stay at Prestige as long as she had. This was the real reason she'd started feeling restless. A year ago, when she'd walked into the private investigation and security agency and talked to Lynn and Casey about a job, she'd told herself working with them was temporary. Her stint with those women was going to be a short-term gig until she got her head together and figured out her next step.

The agency took off, the team grew, and the bond between them wrapped itself around her. Now, these women were her team. They were her friends. Hell, in the last year, they had become her family. And she'd be as pissed off as Lynn was right now if one of them pulled something like this. She didn't blame her teammate for following her, for being angry with her, or for pushing her to be honest about what she had gotten mixed up in.

"We're your team, Meri," Lynn continued. "If you want to do some freelancing, you go searching neighborhood trees for lost cats. You don't put yourself in a situation that clearly has the potential to be dangerous. And you sure as shit don't take clients into your home with nobody to watch your back."

"I didn't take him into my home," Meri snapped. She glanced at the rear passenger window. She had no doubt Troy was tired of being cramped in the small space, so she wanted to make sure he wasn't peering out the window at her. Lowering her voice, she said, "He was standing in my living room when I got home yesterday."

Lynn softened the volume of her voice, but the edge was still there. "Who is he? And don't give me some bullshit story about how he's your childhood friend."

"He worked for me at Lochlin. He was on my team. That kid's parents were murdered in a so-called safe house. He thinks there's a mole on the team. He doesn't know who to turn to, so he grabbed the kid and ran."

"To you."

"Where else would he go, Lynn? He knows he can trust me, and so can you, by the way."

Lynn actually looked repentant for a split second before she nodded. "I know. I'm sorry. I knew you were lying, and it pissed me off. I hit under the belt. I didn't mean it. It was shitty of me to lash out like that. I know I can trust you. But I'm worried. You aren't thinking clearly."

She knew Lynn was right about that, but she tilted her head and dug her heels in anyway. "How so?"

"You're going to run?"

"Yes."

"In a car registered to you through the Department of Transportation? Whose database, I would assume, a savvy security firm can access." Lynn glanced around again, then closed the distance between them, speaking even more softly. "When you told me the truth about who you are and why you wanted to work for me, you also said that the only person you were staying in touch with was your mother. Did she rat you out, or did he find you?"

Meri huffed a sigh.

"If he found you," Lynn stated, "anybody looking hard enough can find you. So what are you going to do? Steal a car when you get out of town? Hijack a train? Because if you buy tickets for any mode of transportation, they'll want to see your ID, which also can be traced back to you."

"I got my go bag with fake IDs."

"What about Prince Charming? Does he have fake IDs? Does he have any way to prove that he didn't kidnap that kid? Which, by the way, it sounds like he did. You think the team at Lochlin aren't looking for him?"

"Someone killed that boy's family," Meri justified. "He didn't kidnap him. He's protecting him."

"Says the guy on the run with a minor."

Meri narrowed her eyes. "I know that *guy*. He wouldn't lie about something like that. He's scared for that boy.

Someone on his team sold out to a major crime family. He's doing what he has to do to protect a kid."

Lynn hesitated but finally nodded. "Okay. If you trust him, then I'll trust him. But you can't disappear on your team, Meri. We can help."

"No, this is—"

"Not an option," Lynn stated firmly. "You don't even know if he's prepared to go underground. If he isn't prepared, that will get you caught."

"He's prepared. He's been at this a long time, Lynn. He's more prepared than a Boy Scout, okay?"

"Great. Then he has a plan. What is it?"

Meri frowned and glanced around the parking lot again. Okay. Fine. Lynn was right. She *wasn't* thinking clearly. That wasn't like her. She was sharper than that. The problem was she'd been thrown off balance, first by Troy's sudden appearance in her new life, then by the confrontation with Lynn earlier. She was acting without thinking ahead, and that was dangerous.

Lynn was right about another thing. Meri was smarter than this. She was better than this. She'd freaked out after Lynn had shown up and responded by acting without thinking. That was the fastest way to get them all killed.

"Come back to the office," Lynn urged. "Let us help you. We'll come up with a plan, a *real* plan. Together. You can't run forever with a child in tow, Meri. Think about the kid."

Meri blew out her breath before nodding her agreement. "Okay. Okay. Thank you. I'm sorry about this morning. I know how it must have looked through your eyes. I wasn't trying to lie to you."

"I know. I'm sorry too. We can talk it out later. Right now let's get that kid somewhere safe."

"Hey," she called when Lynn started around her car. "Have someone get us breakfast. Pancakes for the boy." After climbing back in her car, Meri buckled her seat belt and said, "Change of plans."

"What's going on?" Troy asked from the back seat.

"That was Lynn. She's going to help."

He lifted the blanket enough that when she peered over her shoulder, she met his hardened stare. "You told her?"

"Would you rather I told her and get her on our side, or have one more person on our tail? She can help. She's smart. And she's right. We *need* help."

"For fox sake, Meri."

She creased her brow. "Did you say *fox*?"

"He doesn't cuss in front of me," Logan offered. "He doesn't think I should hear bad words, so he says other words instead."

She grinned. "Good *foxing* thinking, Troy."

Troy had been hesitant to let Meri take him and Logan to her office, but he was impressed by the level of expertise her team exhibited. Lynn called and directed Meri to pull around the back of the building. Once Meri parked, he peered out the window enough to see they were stopped beside a dumpster that was marked as being property of some management company and personal trash was not permitted. Lynn parked right behind them.

Within seconds, three women who looked like they were itching for a fight rushed out of the building to guide Troy and Logan safely inside. They all had the same professional badass air about them that he'd noticed the first time he'd spotted Lynn leaving her car. They knew what they were doing. If anyone had tried to get to Logan, they would have had a small well-prepared army to get through. Once they were inside, a petite redhead locked the door.

"Don't ask their names," Meri ordered. "You don't need to know." She looked at Logan. "Don't say your name, okay?"

"Okay," he said weakly.

A woman with dark hair bent to get eye level with Logan. "Well, you can know my name. It's Joanie. I heard you like pancakes for breakfast. I went and got some for you. You hungry?"

Logan looked up at Troy, who looked at Meri. She nodded, so Troy nodded.

"Go ahead," Troy said. "I'll be close by. Promise."

Logan took Joanie's hand and glanced back twice as she led him away. He had fear in his eyes, but he trusted Troy, which was what made this situation so damn difficult. Troy couldn't make the wrong move where Logan was concerned. The kid had been through enough.

Troy was expecting to join Meri's team as they headed toward a different room, but instead, a blonde grabbed his arm. This woman was different from Lynn as night was to noon. Where Lynn was stiff, likely someone with a military background, this young woman was bouncy and didn't seem to understand the severity of their situation.

"He'll be fine," she assured him. "Joanie is great with

kids. I'm Trista, and I need your picture, then you can join everyone else in the conference room."

"Why? What are you—"

"Fake IDs aren't effective if I use someone else's glamor shot."

"I have IDs in my bag."

Instead of conceding, she pointed at a white wall. Like at the driver's license bureau, he barely looked at the camera in her hand before she snapped a picture. No doubt he looked like hell.

She smiled, baring teeth so white he was nearly blinded. "Perfect."

"Can I see?" Peering at the little digital screen she turned his way, he creased his brow. The lines around his mouth looked deeper than they were a few weeks ago. The dark circles under his eyes spoke to his exhaustion, even after getting a few solid hours of sleep the night before. Yeah. He looked like hell.

"Seriously?"

"Does anyone look pretty on their driver's license?" She jerked her head toward the room where Meri, Lynn, and the petite redhead had disappeared. "Better get in there if you want a say in what happens to you."

"I've worked with Meri before," Troy said. "I gave up that notion the moment I decided to ask for her help."

She laughed. "Have you met Lynn? Because that goes double for her. Go."

The air in the conference room was sucked out like a vacuum the moment Troy walked in. He offered a tilted smile.

"Morning, ladies."

Lynn stepped forward, extending her hand. "Lynn Sanchez."

"Nice to officially meet you," he said, shaking it and deliberately not sharing his name in return.

The redhead glanced up from a laptop she was pecking away at. "Casey Thombert. Any idea how many laws this agency is about to break to protect you?"

Meri and Troy turned toward Lynn. So much for keeping things under wraps.

"They have to know the basics so they can help you," Lynn justified. "Marta might be able to use the fact that you're protecting the kid from a personal security mole to keep you both from going to prison for kidnapping. I think that justifies sharing, don't you?"

"You can leave the room, Marta," Meri offered. "You don't have to get involved in this."

The woman dropped a stack of papers on the table and pulled the pen from her teeth before offering them a bright smile. "Not a chance. I've been dying to do some real security work." She sank into a seat next to Casey.

"I have to have his name, Meri," Casey stated as if Troy wasn't standing right there to answer for himself. "I can't determine if anyone is looking for him if I can't search for him myself."

"None of the people looking for me will be asking the public for help," Troy said.

"What about an Amber Alert for the kiddo?"

Troy shook his head. "No. That would put him in even more danger than he is in already. And, by the way, if any of the people looking for us find out you've helped us, they won't be too kind. If anyone wants to walk out"—he leveled his eyes at the young woman with the messy hair—"now is the time."

Marta looked up, and her smile sagged. She apparently finally caught on that being excited about his plight was not the proper response. In an instant, her face grew serious. "The police will likely detain you at some point," she said. "I'm going to start working on your case now. I'm not going to be your representation, but I can start laying the groundwork for when you do get an attorney. Having the foundation will help them get you released more quickly."

He looked at Meri as the younger woman continued rambling about statutes and loopholes.

"She was going to be a lawyer," Meri said. "She changed course, but she's still brilliant with the law. If you do get charged with anything for this, she'll find a way to get you out of it."

Casey pressed. "How are we supposed to help if we don't have any facts, Meri? Also, can I point out that you can't thoroughly investigate a mole while on the run. You need to stay here. Let us protect you so you can figure this out."

"We can't stay," Troy stated.

Lynn gave him her signature raised-hand move. "You're going to drag that kid around in the shadows, watch your back, and find your mole all alone? That's asking for trouble. You'll make a mistake, you'll get made, and that could get him hurt. You two know how to find a safe house. We know how to protect it. There is no reason to run. Stay and let us help you."

Meri faced him. "She's right. We need a team. One we can trust, and I trust *them*. All of them. There is no mole here. I'd stake my life on it."

"That's great, Meri, but you're asking me to stake *his* life on it." Troy shook his head. "Staying here is too much of a risk."

"So is leaving, but at least here we have backup and a lot more heads to put together to find your mole. Look at you," Meri stated. "You're exhausted. He's terrified. If you two keep going like this, one of you will say or do something that draws attention to you and gets you caught. Let's hunker down and force them to bring the fight to us."

"There's no fight," he said sternly. "There's only me standing between an innocent kid and monsters who wouldn't think twice about putting an end to him."

"No," Meri said. "It's you and me and my team. Let us help you."

He held her gaze. Her dark eyes were all but pleading with him. Finally, he blew out a long breath and looked at the other women in the room.

"I'm Troy Buchanan. That boy is Logan Bantam. His father was a financial advisor, but I suspect he was laundering money, namely for a drug cartel run by the Escobar family. Probably skimming it and took money from the wrong people. He hired Lochlin about four months ago to protect his family. Soon after that, I started to suspect there was a mole on our team. Nothing specific, nothing I can really explain, but I convinced my supervisor to relocate them. I was certain someone was closing in on us, but I didn't have proof until his parents were tortured to death in a safe house. I took the boy to protect him. We have a mole on our team, someone who either killed the Bantams or allowed someone else to. I can only assume that the boy is a target as well. Murderers don't like loose ends, and a potential witness is a very messy loose end. So until I know who that mole is and that they're dealt with accordingly, I will fulfill my obligation as a member of his security detail and keep Logan safe."

"That's all I needed to know," Marta said, apparently satisfied that Troy's decision to take Logan was justified. She started jotting notes on her notepad.

"I need a list of every person who knew where the safe house was," Casey said.

Troy blinked, thinking. "My teammates Randall Gillion and Hank Malony. I've worked with them a long time, but I don't discount that anyone could be bought. The other two were newbies. Deon Waters and Powell Barr." He put his fingers to the bridge of his nose and pinched. "There are some higher-ups as well. I have to think."

Meri put her hand on his arm. "We'll hash it out later and let her know. That's enough for her to get started."

"I'll start with bank accounts and any unexplained purchases," Casey said as she continued typing on her computer. "I'm going to set up a folder in our cloud drive, Meri. You'll be able to access and make notes on anything I add there."

Troy exhaled. "Randall recently bought a new car. A fancy one. He also recently got a new watch. Check into that."

Meri frowned. She didn't say anything, but he could see in her eyes that she didn't want to think the worst of her former teammate. She and Randall had worked together long before Troy joined the team.

Troy didn't want to be suspicious of the man either, but they couldn't risk ignoring something that could be a huge clue because they didn't want to see the truth. In their line of work, even the most trusted of associates had to be handled with a certain amount of caution. They had to remember that.

"We need a place to rent. Some place outside the city so we can keep an eye on you without drawing attention," Lynn said as if what they were doing was an everyday occurrence. Hell, maybe it was. Troy would have to ask Meri what the Prestige team actually did, because they were clearly well prepared to help Logan and him disappear.

"There's plenty of places with acreage for rent," Casey said without looking up from her laptop. "Shawn and I have started thinking about renting since we can't settle on a place to buy. I have a list from my real estate agent right here." She continued tapping away on her laptop. "Some of them even come furnished, which would be perfect."

She turned the screen, and Troy, Meri, and Lynn all leaned closer. Meri took control of the mouse and started scrolling until she stopped at a little house surrounded by woods on two sides, a lake in front, and a long winding driveway that looked like it led to nowhere. The pictures showed a large yard separating the house from the trees. Their protectors would have plenty of places to hide, and anyone trying to sneak up would have to cross the open yard at some point, making them an easy target.

Troy smiled as he looked over the images. If their situation weren't so dire, he'd say that place was paradise. "Looks like a possibility," he said.

Meri finished flipping through the photos. "This is the one. We can put cameras here, here, and here," she said as she pointed to various spots on the property. "How many trail cams do we have?"

"Four, but I'll get more." Lynn pointed at all the spots she thought would be the most logical to put them. She looked at Meri and Troy as if to get their seal of approval.

Troy nodded. "All right. Let's do this. But at the first sign of trouble, Logan and I hit the road."

"First sign," Meri agreed.

"We'll get go bags ready for you in case," Lynn said.

"Just one thing," Troy said. "We can't rent a house. Even with fake IDs. If we pay first- and last-months' rent in cash, we'd do more than raise a few red flags. That much cash screams drug dealers."

"We can get a money order," Marta suggested.

"That's still suspicious," Lynn said without hesitation. "I'll have Justin rent it in his name." She lifted her hand to stop Troy from asking the obvious. "He's a cop. He'll know not to ask questions, and it will put a bit of a buffer between Prestige and the rental agreement."

Trista all but bounced into the room. "Here you go. A whole new you."

Taking the fake license, he looked at the name—Brian Donnelly. That was about as plain a name as someone could get. That would be easily forgotten by anyone who asked to verify his identity.

"And you," she handed one to Meri.

Meri looked from her card to Troy's. Then she frowned at Trista. "*Really?*"

"Brian and Brenda Donnelly." Trista sounded so pleased with herself. "Your son's name...ready? *Brandon*. All your names start with B. Is that not the most adorable thing ever?"

"You have an illness, Trista," Meri said. Even so, she accepted the other documents Trista handed her.

"Passports, drivers licenses, birth certificates, prepaid credit cards." She clasped her hands beneath her chin and batted her eyes. "Marriage certificate. Do you guys need me to buy you rings? Gold? Silver? Platinum?"

"Don't get carried away," Meri warned quietly.

"Do I want to know how you made these in like ten minutes?" Troy asked.

She beamed with obvious pride. "Nope."

Meri tucked the paperwork into the envelope. "We never ask how she does what she does or finds what she finds. Plausible deniability."

"I appreciate the help, but you need to know that someone will come here looking for us," Troy said. "Sooner rather than later. Are you really prepared to lie to the police to protect us?"

"You're our client," Lynn said. "According to Meri, anyway. Might want to give her a dollar to make it official. That will give us a little bit of legal ground to stand on."

"Not much," Meri said. "You're risking everything, Lynn."

She shrugged. "You were going to risk everything first, so it must be worth it."

"There they are," a sweet voice sang out.

Troy turned in time to catch Logan running toward him. He hugged Troy's waist and looked up at Meri. Logan was understandably hesitant to trust, but he already gave Meri the same questioning what-should-I-do look he always gave to Troy. She put her hand on his head and ruffled his wavy hair as she smiled.

"How were your pancakes, buddy?" she asked.

"Good," he answered quietly.

Marta appeared next to Troy. "I think we should find some remote properties to rent. Some under Prestige, some under our names. Anyone looking through our expenses to try to find you will have a lot of digging to do."

"Good thinking," Meri said.

Marta beamed at the compliment. "I'm also going to reserve a car under your name in a few different cities. And make hotel reservations. They won't find you," Marta said, her voice sincere instead of the earlier excitement she'd had. "We won't let them."

For the first time ever that Troy could remember, Meri didn't jerk back when someone went in to hug her. He'd witnessed dozens of witnesses gushing, crying, or being overly friendly. Meri always backed away if they attempted to hug her, but as Marta opened her arms, Meri leaned in. The moment was short but still shocked him. The Meri he knew was harder to crack than the frozen tundra. God knew it took him years to break through her exterior.

"You guys find a hotel to check in to while we get the house rental worked out," Lynn said. "Use my car. We'll get to work on finding something decent for you to drive that we can buy with cash. I'll put yours in your garage."

"Thanks," Meri said as she dug her car keys from her pocket so they could trade.

"Incoming," Trista yelled from the lobby. "Ana Cortez just pulled into the parking lot."

"The front door is locked," Casey called back. "You're going to have to greet her."

Lynn started for the conference room door. "I'll make sure the alley is clear."

"Marta," Meri said, "tell Mrs. Cortez I'm sick and won't be around for a few days but you're taking over her case. You have the notes, right?"

Marta nodded. "Yeah. I read over them yesterday."

"Good." Then to Troy, Meri said, "Let's go."

The women went into action, and some of the apprehension Troy had been feeling eased. Logan held tightly onto Troy's hand as they rushed through the building toward the door where they had entered. After checking the alley, Lynn gestured for them to go. Like before, Troy and Logan stretched on the back seat, and Meri slid in behind the steering wheel.

From his place in the back, Troy watched her continually check the mirrors as she drove. Though he'd been plagued with doubt over the last twenty-four hours, in that moment he knew he had made the right decision. Not just to keep Logan safe and find the damn Lochlin Private Security mole, but to finally get the answers he needed from the woman who had haunted his dreams since the day she'd vanished from his life a year ago.

[4]

Meri drove aimlessly around town, down back roads, and then to a nearby suburb and pulled into a busy gas station to fill up the tank. She was confident they weren't being followed, but if something went down, there would be plenty of witnesses happy to talk about it. She stopped in front of a gas pump and pretended to dig for something while Troy assessed the area from where he still sat in the back seat.

"We're good," he said after looking out every window.

"Can we use the bathroom?" Logan asked.

Meri saw the dread on Troy's face, but he nodded. He couldn't very well make the kid hold his bladder. Then, like the teammates they used to be, they went into action without another word. Troy headed for the station, pulling Logan with him, while Meri watched for any sign of trouble. The moment they were inside, she slid the prepaid credit card Joanie had given her into the pump and filled the tank all while keeping watch. By the time she settled behind the wheel again, Troy was casually glancing around, as if looking for his ride.

Meri started the car, ready to pull away as soon as they were safely inside. He tucked Logan in the back, hopped into the passenger seat, and she lifted her foot from the brake as he was closing the door. She didn't even wait for Troy to secure his seat belt before driving away from the gas station.

She was back on the street within moments. "Let's drive a bit longer before finding a hotel. I want to listen to my messages before we check in, though. I'm hoping Lynn's made progress on the house."

"You made a life for yourself there, huh?" Troy asked.

As restless as she had been lately, she wasn't lying when she told Lynn she didn't want to leave the agency. She couldn't imagine not having those women around her now.

"Yeah. I did. And I like it. Probably more than I should. Emotional attachment in a team can be dangerous."

She realized what she had said and how it must have sounded, but she didn't clarify. She hadn't been wrong. Emotional attachment was dangerous, and she had all the evidence she needed to back that up if he tried to counter her observation.

Instead, he let her comment drop and sounded sincere when he said, "I'm sorry to blow it out of the water for you."

"You didn't. Lynn and I kissed and made up. Things are perfectly fine."

"I brought Lochlin back into your life after you've worked so hard to leave it in the past."

She wasn't sorry he'd come to her for help. In fact, she thought he probably came in the nick of time to save her from going insane with yet another cheating spouse case. Being a private investigator was great, her team was great, but sometimes the cases were so damn boring she couldn't stand it. She had definitely missed the adrenaline rushes that being in the action brought. Or maybe it was the adrenaline rush of something else that she'd missed.

"It's a good thing that you're doing," she said in an attempt to redirect her thoughts. "He's lucky to have someone who cared enough to look out for him. I'm happy to help keep him safe."

The creases in Troy's brow reduced. He even managed a hint of a smile. "He's a good kid. He deserves a better life than what he got stuck with," he added with a whisper.

"A lot of kids do. We'll talk about that later. I still don't have the full story."

"Yeah. We have a lot of things to talk about later."

His words and tone were casual, but Meri understood his real meaning. She didn't want to argue about past decisions.

"I had to go, Troy."

"No, you didn't."

"I failed."

"Because Sarah made a mistake that got her killed?"

"Because I crossed a line that never should have been crossed." She glanced over, making sure he understood the line she mentioned was the one she'd crossed with him.

"I was responsible for that," he said quietly.

"I was your team leader. Your supervisor. The responsibility comes back to me. Always."

"*I* made the move."

Meri gave her head a hard shake, mostly to dislodge the memory before it could take hold and play out in her mind.

"*I* allowed it."

"It's not like we…" He looked at the boy in the back seat who never seemed to miss a beat.

Meri glanced in the mirror. As she suspected, Logan was watching, waiting, analyzing what they were saying. The kid would make a hell of an investigator someday. Though he was timid right now, she had no doubt he'd outgrow that once he wasn't in constant danger. Then it would be his powers of observation that would be dangerous to all those around him.

"Let's finish this later," Troy muttered.

"It's finished," she said.

"The hell it is."

"Hey, Logan?" she called. "You hungry?"

"I'm always hungry," he said with a big smile.

"Me too," Meri responded. "How about I find us someplace to eat?"

"Can I get chicken nuggets?"

Troy frowned at her, and she was certain his displeasure was her blatant use of Logan's stomach to get out of the conversation he was pushing.

"You can get whatever you want, buddy," he said.

Twenty miles and two towns later, Meri pulled off the street to go through a fast-food place. Tapping her fingers on the steering wheel, she counted the seconds tick by as they sat in the line of cars. She hated being trapped like this. No way to move forward, no way to go back.

Troy continued to look around too.

The phrase *sitting ducks* came to her mind as the car

in front of them inched forward. Next time, she would go in and let Troy sit in the car with Logan so they could take off if needed. Caught in an unmoving food line was not a good place to be. Why hadn't she thought of that?

Oh, right. Because she'd been distracted by flashbacks of her and Troy.

Finally, she got to the service window and accepted two bags of food, two large coffees, several bottles of water, and a milk for Logan. She left the restaurant as quickly as she could, itching to get back on the road to put a few miles between them and their latest stop. Then she'd find a place to get a room.

"I bet someone from Lochlin has been watching me," she said as Troy began sorting through the food. She hated the tense silence in the car but didn't know what else to talk about.

"You would have noticed." Troy handed the bagged kid's meal to Logan. "You know all their tricks."

"And they know that. They wouldn't have used them. It's a good thing you didn't know how to call or email me, though. No doubt those are being traced."

Troy's scoff sounded angry and bitter, causing Meri to look his way. Sure enough, he was smirking as he pulled a sandwich from the bag.

"Oh, man," she muttered. "Don't start that again."

"I didn't say a word," he countered.

"You didn't have to, Troy. Jeez. Drop it. I left. You're mad. I know that. Let it go, okay?"

"Don't fight," came a weak plea from the back.

Meri glanced in the mirror while Troy stopped digging for food from the bag.

"We're not fighting, Logan," Troy said, losing the sarcastic tilt to his lips.

"But you were going to," he insisted. "You sounded like Mom and Dad before they start fighting. They fight all the time. I know what fighting sounds like."

Guilt punched Meri in the gut. "I'm sorry. That was my fault. I'm hungry, and sometimes I get irritated when I'm hungry. I didn't mean to sound like I was fighting. I'm sorry," she said to Troy.

"It's okay," he said, joining her in making a show of letting Logan know everything was okay. "I promise," Troy told the boy behind them, "we aren't fighting. And we will *never* fight in front of you."

"Good. Mom and Dad fight all the time," he said again. "Maybe they won't anymore after I go home."

Meri's chest grew so tight she couldn't breathe. *He didn't know.* The kid didn't know he'd never see his parents again. The weight of that knowledge settled over her, and by the look on Troy's face, she guessed that was one of the many things that had been weighing on him as well.

He'd said the day before that he'd been too busy keeping Logan alive to ask about what he did and didn't know, but by the way his face paled, she guessed he simply hadn't known how to ask. But now they knew. Logan was expecting to go home to his parents, and at some point, someone was going to have to explain why he couldn't.

Goddamn it. Poor little guy.

"How are those nuggets?" Meri asked, once again shifting the conversation.

"*So* good," Logan said. "But I really want spaghetti."

"We'll get some the first chance we get," Meri said. "You like garlic bread?"

"Garlic bread is the best."

"I think so too," she said, casting a glance toward Troy.

"Garlic bread is great," he said, but his voice didn't carry the same enthusiasm Meri and Logan had managed. He unwrapped a burger enough that Meri could start eating and handed it to her.

"You guys know what we need to do?" Meri asked. She didn't wait for either to respond, though. "We need to practice using our new names so we don't accidentally say the wrong ones. What's your name?" she asked, looking in the mirror.

Logan answered around his food. "Brandon Donnelly."

"Right. And what's my name?"

"Brenda Donnelly. You're my mom now."

She swallowed the bite of burger she'd taken before clarifying. "Always. I've *always* been your mom."

"And Troy is my dad."

Troy turned in his seat, and she noticed that half his chicken sandwich was already gone. He'd obviously been starving too. "What's my name?"

Logan was quiet for too long.

After several long seconds, Troy gave him the answer. "Brian. I'm your dad, and my name is *Brian*." He looked at Meri. "And you are my wife."

Meri's heart felt like it stopped beating. She had that

stupid little breath-catching thing. That hitch he caused without any effort at all. She hated how he did that to her. No one else had ever had that power over her, and she hated that he did, especially after over a year apart. She gripped the steering wheel and forced herself to swallow so she could remember how to breathe again.

"We've been married for eight years," he pressed on as if he hadn't nearly killed her. There was something in his voice when he said those words. A tenderness that caused her stomach to ache. Or maybe she was hearing something that any woman would hear from her "husband."

She wouldn't really know. She'd managed to avoid having very many serious relationships. Marriage had never been something that interested her, but leave it to Troy to make that kind of long-term commitment suddenly sound so appealing.

She focused on him long enough to see a hint of a smile as he sipped from his coffee, and then she cleared her throat. "Do you remember where we're from, Brandon?"

Logan stopped lifting his milk to his mouth. "Chicago."

Meri nodded. "That's right." She took another bite.

"According to our marriage certificate, we also got married in Chicago. But where did we honeymoon?" Troy asked before stuffing his mouth.

Her stomach twisted. He clearly wasn't intending to let that marriage thing go. "Uh. Vegas," she suggested.

"No," he said around his food. "Too cheesy."

"What?" She chuckled. "Vegas is great. There is no better place in the world for people-watching."

"We did not spend our honeymoon in Vegas. Hawaii," he suggested.

"I've never been to Hawaii," she said. "We should stick with places we know."

"New York. We both know the ins and outs of that place. How many nights did we spend unwinding in Koreatown?"

Damn it. Why did every word that came out of his mouth turn her inside out? She should have seen that coming. There was no place that Meri and Troy knew better together than Koreatown. They loved the food and the atmosphere. They'd almost always walk the streets of the district after having dinner at their favorite restaurant. Their conversations had been effortless.

They'd shared stories of their childhoods and compared the differences between how women and men were treated in their profession. Troy was one of the few men who would get equally as outraged when Meri's qualifications were dismissed because of her gender. He saw it and would speak out against the offenses as freely as she did.

He always came to her defense without acting like some kind of knight in shining armor protecting his damsel. He never treated her like a damsel. That was one of the first things that had earned her respect. And her trust. He clearly found her to be as good of a guard as any man could be.

She had suspected that Randall and Hank had resented her status as lead guard on their team, but she never felt that kind of frustration from Troy. Sarah had still been fairly green when she died on duty, but Meri never sensed the anger Sarah had barely hidden was because of her leader's gender.

Forcing that debate from her mind, she asked, "Do people really honeymoon in New York?" She bit her lip when she heard her accent come through. He, once again, had her off balance, and that was not a good thing. Not for her, and definitely not for the kid in the back seat. Clearing her throat, she worked harder at keeping her enunciation neutral.

"I think that's a myth. There's nothing romantic about New York."

"What?" Troy barked. "Nothing romantic? Central Park."

"People get mugged there every day," she reminded him.

"Lady Liberty."

"Tourists by the hundreds make it impossible to enjoy."

Troy leaned closer with his eyes wide, like he couldn't believe what she was staying. "Broadway."

Meri shrugged. "Broadway has muggings *and* tourists."

"You're crazy," he muttered, falling back into his seat.

She laughed lightly. "*You're* crazy. People who honeymoon in New York City are crazy."

"Where would you go?" He waved his hand. "I don't mean Brenda Donnelly. I mean Meri De Luca…Meri *Osborne*," he corrected. "Where would you go?"

"I don't know. Someplace quiet. I hate crowds. Crowds are bad news. A cabin in the woods somewhere. Like the one Lynn's trying to rent for us."

"I want to go to a cabin in the woods," Logan said. "I've never been to the woods before."

Meri looked over her shoulder at him. Damn. She'd all but forgotten the kid was in the back. She let out a long breath. This was why working with Troy was bad. He didn't have to try to distract her, he did.

"We're working on it," she assured Logan. "In the meantime"—she flipped on her blinker and turned into a parking lot—"let's hang out here for a while."

The chain hotel had secure doors, which didn't provide nearly as much protection as the guests might think, but it was one more obstacle the Escobar family would have to get through. The Lochlin guards would just have to flash their badges, and the person behind the reception desk would have pointed them in the right direction without question.

"You or me?" she asked.

"You," Troy stated. "They may have sent my picture to area hotels."

She ate the last of her hamburger and then reached across him to the glove box and pulled out the baseball cap Lynn always kept there. After wrapping her hair into a wayward bun, she situated the gray hat on her head. For the most part, her dark hair was covered. Someone would really have to be paying attention to her to remember the color. She set her sunglasses on the brim as people tended to do, then checked her face in the mirror.

Nothing about her stood out. She looked like any other exhausted traveler checking into a hotel. Perfect. After verifying she had the proper ID and cash easily accessible, she headed inside to get the Donnelly family a place to rest for the night.

Troy peered out between the curtains, checking the hotel parking lot for anything suspicious. He agreed with Meri that they hadn't been followed, but he didn't doubt for a moment that it wouldn't last long. They'd checked into a local hotel with a car that could be traced back to Meri's colleague. It wouldn't take a genius to connect those two dots.

"Trouble?" Meri asked with a sleep-thickened voice.

He let the curtain fall closed and looked toward the bed where she'd dozed off soon after they'd checked in. She hadn't gotten much sleep the night before, so he'd let her nap. The two of them keeping regular sleeping schedules was not a priority at the moment. They had to take turns being alert while the other rested, and sometimes that meant midafternoon naps.

"No," he said, "I think we're good."

She cleared her throat and eased Logan off her shoulder. Her head had barely hit the pillow before he had curled up beside her and drifted off nearly as fast as she had. As she sat, he clung to her arm as if to prevent her from leaving his side. She patted his back until he relaxed, making sure he stayed asleep.

He didn't intend to watch her so closely, but he was mesmerized by the way she rolled her neck from side to side and stretched before standing. Their gazes locked briefly, but he didn't look away until she did.

"He's a tough little guy, huh?" she asked as she joined Troy by the window.

"Yes, he is."

"Moving on from all of this is going to be hell for him."

Troy let out a slow breath. He had suspected by things that Logan had said that he wasn't fully aware of what had happened to his parents. But then he'd say something else that made Troy think he knew exactly what had happened to them.

Troy sank down in a chair by the table in the room, feeling the weight of Logan's entire existence sitting on his shoulders. "I think he's confused. He doesn't know what he should think, and I don't want to... I don't want to tell him if he hasn't figured it out."

Meri sifted through the little basket of teabags and coffees offered in their room. "He hasn't asked about them?"

"No. Which seems a bit odd."

"Yeah, it does. He knows," she said softly. "He doesn't believe it, or maybe he doesn't understand what it really means."

"That's what I'm thinking. I'm not dumping that on him now."

"I agree," she said as she went about making a cup of coffee. "If he wants to talk about it, we should let him, but we shouldn't bring it up."

He watched her as the coffee brewed, knowing she'd dump three sugar packets into the paper cup because she liked her coffee sweet. She did, and he smiled. She glanced his way and, once again, their gazes locked until she quickly looked away.

"We gotta settle this thing between us, Meri."

She was quiet as the air grew tense around them. "There's nothing to settle."

"Don't do that. Please don't do that. It's just us here. We can finally be honest with each other."

"But it's not just us here." She looked at the bed, and Troy shook his head, not willing to let her use Logan as an excuse not to discuss the giant elephant that had been following them around since she'd found him standing in her living room the day before.

"He's asleep," Troy said. "We can finally talk about this."

Meri scoffed loudly. "I failed my team, so I quit. That's all there is to it. I don't owe you any further explanation."

"You—"

"I was your boss."

"I kissed you," he stated. "I broke protocol. You told me not to. You said it was a mistake. I did it anyway."

She focused on stirring her drink before looking at him. "I said all the right words, but I sure as hell didn't stop you, did I? And Sarah saw us. She had every right to be pissed."

"No, she didn't." Troy ground his teeth and took a breath to soften the edge to his voice. Leaning forward in his seat, he rested his elbows on his knees. "For the millionth time, Meri, I was *not* interested in Sarah. I never was."

Meri set her cup down and turned toward him. "Well, she was interested in you, and I told her there would be no fraternizing on my team. Then she caught us...*fraternizing*. She was right when she called me a hypocrite. I was, and I didn't deserve to be the team leader. She took off on her own without backup because she was mad. She was mad because I screwed up. And she died. She died, Troy," she said with so much strain in her voice, he knew the guilt was still tearing her apart.

He fisted his hands to stop himself from reaching out to her. "You don't know everything, Meri. You left before I could tell you everything."

She stared at him, silently waiting.

"I knew you'd never date a subordinate. You have more integrity than that. But I had wanted to be with you for a long time, and after we kissed, I knew you wanted me too. Let me finish," he said when she opened her mouth. "I went to Director Bruce's office. I was going to ask for a transfer to any other team. I didn't care where as long as I wasn't on *your* team anymore because I didn't want that to be the thing that kept us apart. Sarah came in and said she was happy to see me there. She was planning on turning you in for sexually harassing me."

"Oh my God," Meri said with a miserable-sounding moan.

"However," he continued, "since I was already there, she was happy to stay and be a witness to my complaint. She said between the two of us sharing what had happened, Director Bruce would have no choice but to fire you. I told her I wasn't there to file a complaint against you. I was the one who kissed you, and if anybody got in trouble for harassment, it would be me."

"Nothing is that cut and dry, Troy. They would have had us both on the chopping block."

He ignored Meri's logic. "I told Sarah she needed to let it go and let me transfer so everything could quietly settle down. She couldn't understand why I was protecting you. I didn't want to hurt her, but she wouldn't stop pressing, so I told her I was in love with you. I'd loved you for a long time, and I had finally found the courage to do something about it. I explained that it was the first time I'd kissed you, but I hoped it wasn't the last and...by the way you had responded, I was certain it wouldn't be. She stormed off. That was the last time I saw her."

"It wasn't your fault," Meri said so softly he almost didn't hear her.

"No, it wasn't," he agreed. He couldn't resist closing the space between them any longer. Though he closed the gap, he didn't touch her, despite his need to feel her making his entire body ache. "And it wasn't yours. Sarah let her emotions cloud her judgment and lost sight of her training. She knew better than to go into a potentially dangerous situation alone. We all knew better. She made a choice, a bad choice, and it got her killed. That wasn't our fault."

"She was in love with you, Troy. We both knew that, and we betrayed her."

"We didn't betray her, Meri. I wasn't dating her. I wasn't in love with her." He shrugged. "I couldn't control how she felt or how she responded. I'm sorry she died, but I am not sorry that I finally..." He exhaled loudly. "I'm not sorry I finally let you know that I wanted you. I hate how it ended, but I couldn't hold it in any longer."

Meri lowered her face and exhaled a long, slow breath, obviously processing what he'd told her.

"The only reason I was able to find you so quickly," he said, "is because I started looking for you the day you left."

That got her attention. She jerked her face to him. "Does anybody else know you were looking for me?"

"No. And don't worry. I deleted all my files and wiped

my hard drive when I started to realize I might have to go on the run with Logan. I printed out what I needed and deleted the rest. Don't worry. I covered my tracks."

"Good," she said and then grew quiet again as she focused on her coffee.

Troy thought he could wait her out, but her silence was causing his stomach to ache. "I confessed to being in love with you," he whispered. "Several times, actually."

She turned her face, no longer looking at her drink but still not looking at him. "I heard."

The world shifted beneath his feet. He had hoped—foolishly, it seemed—that she had loved him too. "You didn't love me back."

"I was your—"

"Stop." He took her hands, and she finally met his eyes. "Stop hiding behind your job title."

"I'm not."

"You are. You hid behind it then and you're hiding behind it now. After everything we've been through, I deserve to know if you ever felt the same."

She tilted her head as she frowned at him. "You deserve a swift kick in the ass for thinking transferring off my team would resolve anything. That kind of request raises all kinds of flags, and you know it."

"Are you going to answer my question?"

"You didn't ask a question. You stated what you think you deserve."

He laughed softly. She wasn't going to answer him. They could do this all afternoon long, and she'd never answer him. Dramatically dropping her hands, Troy gave up.

"That's okay. Even if you didn't love me, you wanted me. That much I *do* know."

He went back to the window and peered outside. Nothing. The lot was quiet. He continued to stare outside anyway.

"Do you really think Randall would sell out a client?" she asked after a few minutes. She was a master at diversion. She always had been.

Troy didn't point out that changing the subject didn't change what had happened between them. "I'm leaning that way," he said. He didn't want to think any member of his team would sell out a client, but there was no other way the Bantams could have been found. The Escobars had deep pockets, but Lochlin was good—very good—and they would have known if a client's location had been made. Someone had to share that information.

"Why?"

He found the strength to look at her but couldn't stop the way being so close to her made his heart break a little. He'd told himself a million times that it was the job keeping them apart, but now he had to consider that it wasn't the job. She didn't love him like he had loved her. She'd lusted after him. And it had ended there for her.

He pushed the disappointment down and focused on her question. "The new watch and car that I mentioned, for starters. Also, he's dating a woman that he hasn't told anyone on the team about. I found out when I started investigating the team. We tell each other everything. Okay...*almost* everything. But he never told me about her."

"For how long?"

Troy rolled the information he'd been gathering through his mind. "About four months."

"How long were they clients?" she asked, referencing Logan's family's stay under Lochlin's protection.

"Four months."

Meri heaved a sigh. There was no denying the coincidence of that. "Shit."

"Yeah."

"How many times did I tell you guys not to think with your"—she glanced at the boy still sleeping on the bed, then softly added—"private parts. You men never listen."

Troy chuckled. He could say the same thing about women, but he didn't. "Randall's got three years until he can retire, yet he never made team leader. He never even made it to second in command. He watched me climb the ranks of our team, but he never moved forward."

"He didn't have it in him to be a leader. He didn't think things through. He would have missed something, made a mistake, and gotten someone killed."

"I'm not disagreeing," Troy said. Randall was smart and dedicated, but he was overly confident in his abilities. Though he made rash decisions without considering all the options, he never would have had the guts to grab Logan and run. He would have gone through the system, played by the rules, and possibly put Logan in even more danger. "I'm simply pointing out," Troy continued, "that sometimes a guy works his entire life for something that he never gets, and it can make him bitter. And angry. And anger makes for bad decisions."

"Damn it," Meri said. "He's a good guy. I'd hate to think he blew his career for money."

"Money makes people do stupid things. So does sexual attraction."

She shot her gaze at him, and he grinned. She might not have loved him in return, but their lust had been strong. He would cling to that if it was all he had.

"Jesus, you're incorrigible," she muttered before grabbing her bag and walking toward the bathroom.

Troy laughed. He couldn't help himself. They might be in danger and on the run, but he had Meri at his side again. That made the rest of the situation—even accepting that his affections had been one-sided—more tolerable.

[5]

MERI WRAPPED a stiff towel around her torso and tucked the end in. As she used another towel to dry her hair, she couldn't ignore how her muscles were already starting to stiffen again. The long hot shower had done little to ease her tension. She'd like to blame the stress on the long day or Logan's predicament, but she knew the reason she was so tense.

Troy said he'd been in love with her when they worked together. Which she'd known. She'd known long before that day over a year ago when he'd muttered that losing his job was worth the risk as he grabbed her sides and yanked her to him. All the other members of their team had rushed off to grab an early lunch after their morning meeting had ended.

Troy had lingered, as he tended to do. She had been far too aware of him all during the meeting, but having him dawdle when everyone else was gone, knowing they were alone in the room, made it hard for her to focus on gathering her notes. Then he'd closed the door as he said he had something he needed to talk to Meri about.

The clicking of the door sounded like thunder, signaling the start of a storm.

Her heart nearly burst because she knew—or strongly suspected—what he was going to say. There was no way they could keep denying what they both obviously knew. The attraction between them was electric and only getting stronger. They had to find a way to control it before someone else started feeling the shocks.

They couldn't keep ignoring what was happening between them, but they couldn't act on it either. Meri had been trying to figure out what the hell to do. Actually, she had known for some time what she had to do—she simply didn't want to do it. She had to put an end to all of their non-business-related interactions. She had to go back to treating him like a subordinate and less like the friend he'd become.

She was going to tell him that. She was going to draw the line in the sand. But then he'd said he didn't care about his job and pulled her to him. She had managed to tell him that they shouldn't be doing that before he'd pressed his mouth to hers.

In that moment, she stopped caring about agency rules and professional integrity. The world had stopped turning. Her heart had stopped beating. She couldn't breathe. All that mattered was Troy and how absolutely perfect having his arms around her felt. How kissing him was even better than she'd fantasized. And how she'd never wanted that moment to end.

But it had ended. Abruptly. Sarah walked in and

slammed the door behind her so hard the pictures on the wall had shaken as if they, too, felt her rage.

Meri tried to force the memory from her mind, but as she dressed in leggings and a tank top, she heard every vicious—and true—word Sarah had screamed at her.

Troy had attempted to take the blame, but Sarah wasn't buying it. Meri didn't blame her. Meri was the superior. The blame was hers. Always. After Sarah stormed out, Troy had put his hand to Meri's face and promised everything was going to be fine. And then he left Meri alone to come to terms with how much she'd screwed everything up in those few passionate seconds.

The next time she had seen Troy, her team was watching the police investigate the scene of Sarah's murder. Troy had called Meri several times after that. He'd come to her home and knocked on the door. He had even tried to corner her at the funeral. She'd avoided him, ignored him, and then she'd left him.

Without a word.

Her disappearing act hadn't been fair to Troy, but she was certain it had been necessary to save him. She was going to go down in flames if anyone found out about the confrontation that had occurred prior to Sarah's death. She wasn't about to take Troy down with her. If she left, they could place the blame on her. Troy would be safe.

She didn't know where she was going or what she was going to do, but as soon as she got home after Sarah's funeral, she had changed her clothes and grabbed her go bag and as many extra clothes as she could fit into her duffel bag.

She'd called her mom on the way out of town and told

her that she would hire someone to pack the rest of her belongings and put them in storage. Her mom had tried to change her mind, of course, but Meri needed time and space to think.

Once she landed in a new city, she had gone about covering her tracks enough to not be followed. Looking back, she realized she could have done a lot better. She had known Troy would come looking for her. And she'd left enough breadcrumbs for him to follow.

She hadn't meant for her departure to be a test, but maybe, on some unconscious level, it was. Maybe she wanted to see if he cared enough to find her. She'd always hated games like that, but perhaps she'd played one without intending to. The years of experience at Lochlin Private Security certainly had given her the skills to go completely underground, but she hadn't done that. She'd used a family name, kept her first name, and worked within a similar industry.

She certainly wouldn't have allowed a witness to do any of those things. The slate could have been wiped clean to make it next to impossible for Troy to follow her. She'd left so his job would be secure. But she'd made it easy enough for him to locate her if he wanted to.

It had only taken a year and a kid in crisis for him to do so.

Easing the door open, she tip-toed into the area of the room where two queen beds filled most of the space. Logan was still asleep, and she wondered if maybe they should wake him up. She didn't know much about parenting, but she did know that if they let him sleep too long now, he wouldn't want to sleep at night.

Everything else in his life was spiraling out of control. They should do their best to keep him on a regular schedule. But then she looked at Troy, sitting at the table, this time with papers spread in front of him. She didn't doubt those were the notes he had told her he'd been compiling before going on the run.

She'd tossed her career away because she didn't want to see him delegated to some desk job he'd hate or get fired from the agency. He was a good marshal. He was strong and smart. Smart enough to know the team had been compromised. Smart enough to know that he needed to print out and delete the digital copies of his evidence so it couldn't be seen by the wrong person.

He'd moved up the ranks to become the leader of the team she'd left behind. She was proud of him. She always knew he had it in him to be a good leader. Leaders had to make tough decisions. Like leaving for the betterment of her team or going into hiding with a child whose life was in danger.

The exhaustion Troy felt was so obvious, and not in his sagging shoulders and the bags under his eyes, but the determination in him never wavered. He had always been honorable. He'd always been strong and brave. He'd always had some magnetic force about him that she hadn't been able to ignore. She'd felt the pull between them the first time they'd met. She'd known then he was going to be her undoing. She'd accepted that long before he'd kissed her.

He had been worth it. Leaving her job, losing her career,

walking away from her life had been worth that one moment. She'd been clinging to the memory for a year. She had dated other men in a vain attempt at letting Troy go, but they'd never come close to erasing him from her mind. She hadn't allowed them to because she knew he would come for her. She knew he wouldn't give up that easily.

So, she guessed, she had played a game with him. She'd tested to see if he was worth the life she'd lost for him. She knew now, watching him struggling with the fact that he had to dissect his own team to protect Logan, that he was. He was worth everything.

"That's some pretty heavy thinking going on over there," Troy said. "What's going through your head?"

She smirked. "I was thinking that…" She stopped herself before she could give him her usual sarcastic retort. He had given her the truth. He deserved to hear hers. "I could have done better at covering my tracks. I could have made it harder for you to find me."

"It took me a year."

"If I'd put more effort into it, you wouldn't even be close. Yet here you are."

A lazy grin curved his lips as he continued looking at his research. "Maybe I'm smarter than you."

"Ha. That will never happen."

He still didn't look at her, and she realized his focus on his papers was deliberate. He clearly didn't want her reading his face, as she could so easily do.

"So, what you're saying," he said, "is that the only reason I won is because you let me."

"Yeah. I guess that's what I'm saying."

"And why would you let me win?"

She held her breath, swallowed hard, then blurted, "Because I was in love with you too, and I was terrified of what that meant for both of us. I didn't want us losing our careers over something that might or might not work out."

Troy froze, his hand hovering over the page he was about to pick up as he slowly turned his face up to her. "I thought so," he said, and his smile spread. "But it's damn good to hear you say it."

A strange sense of peace washed over her, like she'd finally confessed the deepest, darkest secret that had been weighing on her soul.

"I couldn't let you throw your life away, Troy."

He sat back, no longer pretending to be distracted by his papers. "So you threw yours away instead?"

She nodded. "The truth would have come out if I'd stayed. There would have been an internal investigation, and every move we'd ever made would have been scrutinized. We both would have been dragged through the mud, and then we would have been fired. Our careers would have ended, and...and the reality is, we probably wouldn't have survived that. Together, I mean. We would have been torn apart."

"So you thought it was your responsibility to take the fall."

"It was."

He slid his chair back and stood, slowly walking toward her. "You don't always have to take the blame, Meri. Other people screw up sometimes too. Me kissing you was inevitable. Me kissing you in a conference room at the office was stupid. I just...I couldn't hold my feelings in for one more minute. That was on me."

He stopped in front of her, and she filled with equal parts dread and anticipation. He was going to kiss her again. He was going to pull her to him like he'd done the last time. He was going to put his mouth on hers. And then she was going to lose herself again. At least this time, there was nothing to stop them from acting on the attraction between them.

He slithered his arms around her and pulled her into an embrace so tight she couldn't breathe. Not that she wanted to. Troy lifted her several inches off the floor and carried her to the little alcove with the sink, where he eased her feet to the dark-green carpeting, but he didn't release his hold as he leaned down.

Without hesitation, he crushed his mouth against hers. She could have sworn the world swallowed them whole. Nothing else existed. Time stood still. His heat enveloped her, and she finally allowed herself to feel beyond the physical attraction they'd shared from day one. Beyond the lust, she felt love.

Love for him and loved by him.

She'd known for months before he'd acted on what they were feeling that they had somehow fallen in love with each other without even having touched intimately. What they felt was so much deeper than physical connection.

Feeling his warmth around her now, she felt the same. She didn't doubt for a moment that he was telling her the truth. He loved her. And now that he was standing here, she couldn't deny the other half of their truth—she loved him too.

"I'm sorry," she said when he finally pulled back for a breath. "I should have told you I was leaving."

"It doesn't matter now." He held her face like he'd done before he'd followed Sarah that day. His skin on hers was like fire lighting a fuse. Sparks practically danced along her flesh. "This is what matters. We're here. And we're going to find out who the mole is and we're going to get Logan back to safety. And then we're going to be together like we should have been all this time."

Meri opened her mouth, but he hushed her with a stern look.

"Don't argue with me," he warned.

She grinned. "I was simply going to say that's the best plan I've heard from you all day."

"Hey," he said with mock offense.

She softly laughed as she wrapped her arms around his neck and pulled him closer. "I knew I was going to hurt you when I left, but I had to do what I could to protect you. I didn't want you to lose your job."

"I know. I would have done the same thing if I'd been in your position. I would have left too. I knew why you disappeared. I was pissed, but I understood." Stroking his hand over her hair, he smiled. "I love you, Meri. Still."

Her heart felt lighter, like the burden she'd been carrying for so long was lifting. "I love you. *Still.*" Resting her head on his shoulder, she closed her eyes and soaked in the feel of him. She had missed him so much more than she'd allowed herself to think about.

She never would have considered herself one of those clingy women who wanted to crawl inside her man, but in that moment, she wouldn't have minded if Troy never let her go. She'd gone too long without feeling his arms around her.

Troy threaded his fingers through her hair as he kissed the top of her head. His touch was comforting and filled some of the void she'd been feeling, but she wanted more. So much more. Tilting her head back, she caught his mouth with hers again and parted her lips, ready to give him a real, deep kiss.

"Are you guys really married now?"

Troy jerked away from Meri as he turned, and they both looked at Logan standing a few feet from them. Neither seemed to know how long he had been standing there.

"I thought you were asleep," Troy said as Meri wiped her mouth.

"I got thirsty," Logan stated as if his predicament should be the most obvious thing in the world. "Did you get married? For real?"

"No," Troy said. "We were just…"

"We're very good friends," Meri offered.

Logan narrowed his eyes. "I saw my dad kiss my nanny like that once. When I asked Mom why he did that, she got mad. She said only married people are supposed to kiss like that. Then she yelled at my dad, and I had to get a new nanny."

Meri felt Troy stiffen beside her. Clearly he too was surprised by this revelation.

"Your dad…" she asked hesitantly, "kissed the nanny?"

Logan nodded. "Mom said only married people kiss like that. If you aren't married, you shouldn't kiss like that."

"Uh. You know what," Meri said, "that's true, but since

Troy and I are really good friends and…and…" Shit, she was about to manipulate a kid. "And since we are *pretending* to be married, you know…it's okay that we kissed like that."

Logan stared at her for a few seconds before accepting her answer. "Can I have some water?"

Meri unwrapped a plastic cup and filled it from the tap as Troy headed back into the sleeping area of the room. After handing the drink to Logan, she patted his head.

"Put the cup back on the sink when you're done," she said, and then she followed Troy to the table where he started scribbling on the notes he'd been poring over before she had disturbed him.

"What are you thinking?" she asked.

"Maybe I'm wrong. Maybe the mole wasn't on our team. Maybe Richard Bantam was so hot for the nanny that *he* was the leak. If he told her where he was so they could try to hook up…"

"She could have told whoever was after them," Meri said, finishing his thought. "It wouldn't be the first time a criminal infiltrated the lives of people to keep an eye on them."

Troy shrugged. "Women can be the bad guy too, remember? I knew in my gut something was wrong, but that doesn't mean that something was wrong with our team. I could have been picking up something from Richard. He had been warned against sharing his location."

"I'll text Lynn," Meri said. "We need whatever she can find on this woman. I don't suppose you know her name? Do you know if she was ever interviewed?"

"No. This is the first I've heard of her, but it makes sense. Sharon Bantam was dramatic like that. I can see her losing her mind in front of everyone, including Logan. More than once we had to remind her that her kid was in the house to calm her down. His parents were never very good at censoring themselves, even if he was in the room."

"No wonder he got so upset at the thought of us fighting. Poor baby."

"Can we go outside?" Logan asked, interrupting their muted discussion. When neither grownup answered, he added, "Can we? *Please?* I want to play outside."

Meri didn't have to ask the last time he was allowed to play outside. The answer was likely to be before his family were hidden away by Lochlin. Trips to the park weren't high on the activity list for people whose lives were in danger.

"You know what. There's a pool downstairs," she offered. "I bet we could—"

"I don't swim." The pout in his voice was nearly enough to crush the high she was still riding from kissing Troy.

"Okay. Well, we should be in a house by tomorrow—"

His little lip trembled, and tears flashed in his eyes. "I never get to go outside."

She put her hand on his head and looked at Troy. He had that guilt-torn ache in his eyes again. She didn't have to be a mind reader to see that he was worried he was doing even more damage to the kid in his attempt to protect him.

She tried to think of alternatives. Lynn had a decent-sized back yard, but there weren't many areas that hadn't been covered in landscaping of some kind. She and Justin had filled what was once a nice wide open grassy space with brick tiers, plants, and sculptures.

Joanie's boyfriend had a nice yard, but he worked from

home, and the last thing Meri wanted was for him to see Logan.

The rest of the Prestige team lived in apartments.

However, Meri was familiar enough with the neighborhoods surrounding the hotel where they were staying to know there were lots of small parks for the suburban residents. Small enough to keep a close eye on Logan while watching for danger.

"I think we're safe enough to find a park," Meri whispered to Troy. "Let's give him ten minutes. Just enough time to run around."

He was about to say no—Meri saw it on his lips, and she didn't blame him—but she was confident they hadn't been followed.

"Please," Logan practically begged. "I wanna go outside, Troy."

"Ten minutes," Meri said.

"Only," Troy stated, "and I mean *only* if your team is there to play lookout."

"Yes!" Logan did a little fist-pump that made Meri laugh as she pulled her burner phone from her pocket to see if she could set up a play date with the Prestige team.

"I'm not crazy about this," Troy said as Meri parked the car. He eyed the playground structure. Though most of it was open, the big yellow slide was covered from the top almost to the wide bottom.

"You stick close to him," Meri said. "The rest of us will be the lookouts."

Troy glanced at Logan grinning as the little guy stared out the window.

"He needs to run and play, Troy," Meri said. "For a few minutes. Casey's on the bench to the north. Marta is doing yoga to the west. Joanie is reading to the south. And I'm going to be standing at the east. We have you surrounded. It's going to be fine."

The only reason Lynn wasn't present was because she was busy getting a house rented for the "Donnelly" family. Trista was holding down the fort back at the office according to Meri. The rest of the team was there, though. Blending in like the professionals he'd realized they were.

Troy turned in his seat. "Who am I?"

Logan stopped staring out the window and focused on Troy. "Dad."

"Who is she?"

"Mom."

"And who are you?" Troy asked.

"Brandon."

Meri said, "When we say it's time to go, you snap to. No whining or complaining. Got it?"

"Got it." He bounced in his seat. "Can we go play now?"

"Let's go play," Troy said after taking another look around. He stayed close as Logan darted straight toward that damn slide. He waited at the bottom, keeping a close eye on the boy's trek up the metal structure while also scanning the area.

The only other parents in the area were women. But, as

Meri loved to remind him, women could be bad too. Both sat on a bench, chatting and sipping from paper cups while three kids close to Logan's age chased each other around the grassy area on the other side of the rubber-mulched circle that contained swings.

"Watch this," Logan called, pulling Troy's attention back to him.

He looked up in time to see Logan swing from a bar and launch himself into the slide. Seconds later, he tumbled out at the bottom, laughing in a way that Troy hadn't heard in weeks.

Troy smiled. "Good job, buddy."

"Can I go on the monkey bars?"

"Sure thing." The words were barely out of Troy's mouth before Logan was running off again. Troy took big steps but made a point not to rush too quickly. He didn't want to draw the attention of the moms on the bench. He wanted to be attentive but not hover. He suspected that parents hovering over six-year-olds on the playground would draw scrutiny of other parents. Scrutiny meant they would be watching, and Troy didn't want anyone other than the Prestige team to be aware of them.

Logan reached the other side of the set of bars and jumped down. The instant his feet hit the ground, he was off again. He went from area to area without slowing down. The slide, the swings, the monkey bars, then he'd start all over again. He didn't stop running, laughing, or intentionally falling to the ground as he came out of the slide until Meri's yell cut through the air.

"Brian!"

Her voice wasn't panicked, but she wouldn't have called out unless something was wrong. Spinning at the sound of his fake name, Troy caught Meri staring at him. A chill ran down his spine when he noticed her hand hovering over her hip where she kept her gun.

He didn't know what she was on to, but he called for "Brandon" to come back. Logan turned but didn't come to him immediately like he'd been told to do. His eyes were filled with questions.

It was then that Troy noticed two men closing in on the playground. There were no kids with them, and one was carrying a golf bag over his shoulder.

A golf bag? Coming toward a playground?

Hell no. That son of a bitch was hiding guns in that bag. Troy's stomach dropped to the ground. He immediately took an assessment of the area to determine the best course of action. Joanie had set her book aside and was standing, ready to act if needed. Marta was no longer bending herself like a pretzel but was also standing with her hand inside a backpack, reaching for a gun undoubtedly. Casey was already on the move, walking at a brisk pace to close the distance between her and the men.

"*Brandon*," Troy said more sternly. "Now."

When Logan ran to him, Troy scooped him up and rushed toward Meri. Not running, but he was moving fast.

Meri was ready to pull her gun. Her hand was on the butt, and she had already released the button on her holster. She could have drawn her weapon and been firing in less than a second. Troy passed her, not slowing his stride. By the time he reached the car, she was coming up behind him. He opened the back door and practically tossed Logan in.

As Meri got behind the wheel, Troy slid into the back seat next to Logan. She shoved the key into the ignition switch and turned it as the kids that had been running in circles stopped chasing each other and headed toward the suspicious men.

The other women he was counting on to keep Logan safe eased but didn't relax. They were still ready to act if needed.

It wasn't.

Dads. They were just dads. The playground must have been adjacent to a course, and these men were joining their families for a play date after a round of golf. Even so—even if their reasons were justified—Troy was too on edge to let Logan back out of the car.

Meri must have been as well. She started the engine and pulled away. Damn it. She was right. The kid needed to be a kid, but not if it was going to cost him his life.

As they left the park and turned onto a two-lane street that would take them back to the hotel, Troy focused on getting his adrenaline rush under control.

In the driver's seat, Meri continued glancing around, obviously double-checking that they weren't being followed.

"Are we okay?" Logan asked, his voice trembling.

"We're fine," Troy said with a happy tone that nobody in the car actually felt. He patted his knee as he caught Meri's eye in the mirror. "We're fine," he said to Meri. "But we can't do that again. It's too risky."

"I'm sorry, Troy," Logan said. "I wanted to play."

"It's not your fault, buddy," he said.

"Did you burn off some energy?" Meri asked.

Logan answered by nodding his head, all his enthusiasm gone.

"You looked awesome going down that slide," Meri said.

The only sound from Logan was a sniffle. Damn it. Troy hadn't meant to make him cry. He didn't know what to say to make it better.

"Are you mad at me?" Logan asked.

"No," Troy answered. "Not at all. I got scared for a minute because I'm so worried about you. But you're okay. Everybody's okay. Lynn is trying really hard to find us a house with a yard. Once we get there, you can go play outside."

"I want to go home," Logan said with a trembling voice.

Troy's heart freaking broke in a way that he'd never felt before. This was too much for a kid to deal with.

"I know you do," he said. "But you can't right now. You can't. I'm so sorry about that."

The rest of the ride was quiet except for the occasional sniffle from Logan. Troy felt like absolute shit. As Meri parked, he looked at the door that would lead them into the hotel.

"You have your key card handy?" he asked.

"Got it," Meri answered. She climbed from the car and headed for the door. As soon as she had it open, Troy and Logan would follow.

"I didn't mean to scare you," Troy said as he watched her head for the door. "I got worried, and it made me upset. But not at you, okay?"

"Okay," Logan said.

As Meri yanked on the door, he climbed from the car and pulled Logan out with him. Once they were inside the hotel, they rushed up the stairs to the second floor. Meri took the lead to get the room door open. As soon as they were inside, she pulled Logan against her while Troy did a quick search of the room.

"Clear," he said from the bathroom before joining them in the bedroom.

Logan kicked his shoes off, pouting ever so slightly, as he dropped into a chair at the table.

"Know what I'm going to do?" Meri said. "I'm going to call Joanie and have her bring us spaghetti. There's an Italian restaurant not far from here. She can pick it up for us."

Troy smiled at the way the happiness finally returned to Logan's eyes. "Only if she brings garlic bread too."

Logan laughed. "I love spaghetti."

Meri dug her phone from her pocket and nodded when Troy thanked her for the good idea. She left the room to make the call, so he suspected she was also verifying that the men at the park hadn't been after them. Hopefully, she would get confirmation that they had a house too. And maybe she could even see if one of the Prestige team had found the mole. That'd be great.

In fact, that'd be perfect. He could hand Logan back to the government knowing he was going to be safe, and he could get back to talking about the future he and Meri had never had a chance to plan.

[6]

Meri was convinced there couldn't be a home better suited for her and Troy's needs. Usually, a neighborhood home would be ideal for hiding a family, but with Lochlin being on the lookout for Troy and Logan, the solitude of the rural house was safer.

More so, Logan was free to scream and laugh as he ran around the open yard. They were surrounded by trees on three sides and a pond on the other. Lynn had spent hours adding cameras and sensors around the property. Any trespasser would set off an alarm somewhere on their way to the small house.

Meri peered out the window above the kitchen sink at Logan when another yelp filled the air. Marta was unexpectedly great with kids. Joanie was there too, monitoring the tree line while Marta played a game to keep her close to the kid who finally got to act like a kid.

Though the property was secure and they all could relax a bit more, none of them were foolish enough to completely let their guard down. They weren't just hiding Logan from a mole. There was a drug cartel out there that was ultimately responsible for the death of his parents. Logan was likely still on their target list as well.

A shiver ran down Meri's spine, but not the scary kind—the kind that sent a thrill through her and settled low in her stomach. She sensed Troy before he stepped to her side. She'd had to ignore those subtle responses her body had toward him for so long that they were nearly overwhelming now that she had allowed herself to feel them. Just having him so close made her heart beat faster, but when he casually rested his hand on the small of her back, she nearly swayed on her feet.

"He's having fun," she said, trying to ground herself so she didn't throw herself into Troy's arms and all but beg him to take her.

"Good. He deserves some fun." He gently pulled her closer and whispered in her ear, "So do we."

A few seconds passed before Meri caught his innuendo. She widened her eyes and gasped, causing him to throw his head back and laugh.

Holy shit. She hadn't heard the man laugh like that since the last time they'd met at their restaurant in Koreatown. The sound was like a balm soothing her. The urge to slide into his arms was strong, and she might have given in if the sound of incoming voices hadn't indicated that Lynn and Trista were done setting up the cameras in the other rooms.

Meri turned from the window and away from Troy's hand on her back in time to catch Trista grin as if she'd known exactly what had been whispered moments before.

Lynn didn't look nearly as amused. When Trista turned to go out the back door to join Marta and Joanie outside, Lynn leveled her eyes at Meri.

"Surveillance is all set up," Lynn said. "Let me show you how to use it."

"There's no need for that," Meri said. "I've been through this a few times."

"Let me show you anyway," she said, jerking her head toward the spiral staircase that led to the loft where there were several monitors on a desk. Each one showed different areas around the property that were being watched at all times.

"What is going on between you and Troy?" Lynn asked the moment Meri stepped onto the carpet upstairs.

Her question was not the girly gossip tone that Trista would have used. Or the suggestive, husky tone that she would have gotten from Joanie or Casey. Lynn's question was stern and unamused. Demanding if not outright accusatory.

"What?" Meri asked as if she didn't know exactly what Lynn was asking.

Lynn simply lifted her brow and pressed her lips together.

Meri glanced at the monitors to break the intense stare from her boss and friend. "We were friends before I left Lochlin Private Security."

"Friends, Meri? Or *friends*?"

Meri was not used to being the center of Lynn's scrutiny, and she didn't like it. She and Lynn were close. This attack took Meri by surprise and set her already frayed nerves on fire. "Friends. I left before it could become more. Okay?"

"Is this going to be a distraction?"

"No."

"Meri, if—"

The slight sense of offense Meri felt surged. "Have I ever questioned your ability to protect someone?"

"That boy's parents were murdered. Whoever did that can only assume he saw something. I doubt they'll ask you nicely to get out of the way if you come between them and their target."

Meri scoffed. "I'm not going to put myself, Troy, or Logan at risk to get laid."

"That's not what I meant."

Narrowing her eyes, Meri asked between gritted teeth, "Then what did you mean?"

Lynn looked at the monitors for a few long seconds. When she focused on Meri again, her eyes were softer. "Troy is the real reason you left New York, isn't he?"

"I left because my teammate got killed, and I was responsible."

"I don't want to lose you. I'm worried that you aren't thinking clearly with this case. If you need one of us to pose as Brenda Donnelly—"

"I don't."

It was obvious that Lynn didn't believe her. Instead of arguing further, her boss nodded and walked down the stairs. Meri shook her head in an attempt to free herself of the disagreement before she followed Lynn. By the time she reached the open living area, Lynn was going out the back door.

"What was that?" Troy asked the second the door closed.

Meri drew a deep breath. "I've worked for her for over a year now. She's never questioned my competency before. She's done it twice in the last forty-eight hours. Who the fuck does she think—"

"Never get emotionally attached," Troy stated, cutting off her rant. "That's one of the many things that you beat over our heads. You make mistakes when your emotions get involved. She'd have to be blind not to realize we have feelings for each other." He smiled and shrugged. "That's probably my fault. I think my poker face is slipping. She's your boss, Meri. And she's worried that if something goes down, you're going to be thinking with your heart instead of your head. Which, in case you've forgotten what happened to Sarah, can get you killed."

Meri drew a deep breath as she considered his words. Damn it. Lynn had a point, and she was right to be concerned. Meri would be concerned if she were in Lynn's shoes.

"Leave it to you to turn my life upside down," she said, causing him to grin.

Turning, she marched for the door, taking long strides until she stopped at Lynn's side on the edge of the backyard.

"Sarah had a thing for Troy. I told her to get over it or transfer to another team because getting emotionally involved with a teammate is dangerous. What I didn't tell her was that Troy and I were...*feeling* things for each other. We weren't together," she clarified, "but we definitely were spending more time together outside of work than we should have been. I cared about him. I *loved* him," she admitted. "But there was a professional line, and I wasn't about to cross it. But one day, Troy did. He kissed me. Sarah saw us, and she was furious at us—at me, to be honest. After unleashing on me, she took off to check on a client by herself. She wasn't paying attention to her surroundings and ended up dead. I quit before an investigation took me *and* Troy down. He told me last night that he still loves me." She couldn't help the smile that touched her lips. "I still love him too, Lynn. But I'm not going to let that interfere with keeping Logan safe or with finding out who the Lochlin mole is. I can still do my job, not get myself killed, and be human."

"I know." Lynn frowned as she watched Marta and Logan running through the yard. "That's not what I meant when I said I don't want to lose you."

"What did you mean, then?"

"Something has been off with you for a while now," Lynn said. "We've all seen it, and we've all wondered what was going on. It was him, wasn't it? You were missing Troy."

Meri watched Logan scream and dramatically throw himself to the ground as Marta threatened to tickle him. Really, Meri was using the distraction to consider Lynn's assessment.

"Yeah, I think so. I left Troy without a word despite how close we had gotten. For a long time, I was able to convince myself that was the best thing for him, but lately I've been doubting my actions. I was selfish when I told Sarah she couldn't pursue a relationship with Troy, and I was selfish when I left him without explanation. I never meant to, but my feelings for Troy hurt Sarah, and then my decision to disappear hurt Troy. Lately I've been realizing how much I hurt myself too."

"It's never an easy situation when teammates get involved, but it sounds like you did the best you could given the circumstances."

"Yeah, I've been telling myself that lie for a year now, Lynn. I'm not sure I buy it anymore. I should have broken up my team before things got messy. I saw the trainwreck that was coming, I didn't want to have to make up excuses to the director why I needed a new team. I couldn't very well tell him some soap opera love triangle was forming. That would have gotten us all in trouble."

"He's going to leave when this is over, Meri. He's going to go back to his life and his job. You're going to go with him, aren't you?"

Meri hadn't considered much beyond protecting Logan. But she did know whatever came next, she wanted to be with Troy.

"I don't know. I mean, we could all very well end up in prison for kidnapping, so..." She smiled when Lynn let out a soft laugh. "I don't know how to answer that, but even if I did go back to New York with him, you're not losing me."

"But you won't be here. You won't be part of Prestige anymore."

A lump rose to Meri's throat. "Lynn Sanchez, you're a big fucking teddy bear," she teased to lighten the moment.

Lynn chuckled and shook her head. "Tell anyone else, and I'll shoot you myself."

Meri looked to the window where Troy was watching

over the backyard. "I don't know what happens next, but I do know that I missed him," she confessed. "I felt like I couldn't breathe sometimes from missing him."

"Does he feel the same?"

"I think so."

Lynn took a deep breath and let it out with a loud sigh. "Well, you're getting a second chance with him now. You have to embrace it. If that means you leave Prestige to go home, then that's what you have to do. As much as I want you here, your happiness is more important."

"Would you leave us for Justin?"

Lynn smiled and then nodded. "Yeah. If I had to. But we'd still be family."

"We'll always be family."

"Yeah, okay," Lynn stated dismissively. "This is getting way too touchy-feely for me. I'm going to go check the perimeter again. By the way," she said walking away, "Trista has convinced me to promote her to be in security instead of running the office. You get to train her."

Meri opened her mouth, intent on sarcastically countering, but the idea actually appealed to her in a way that she wasn't expecting. She'd spent so much of her life shut down, keeping everyone as far away as she could because of the risks of getting too invested. Suddenly she didn't want that any longer. She wanted to feel the connection she had with her team. She wanted the love she felt for Troy, the love she'd denied them both long before quitting Lochlin Private Security.

"Yeah," she said as her smile spread. "Keep pissing me off and see how that goes."

Lynn had barely walked away before Marta stopped chasing Logan and joined Meri at the edge of the yard.

"Everything okay?" Marta asked, sounding a bit breathless from chasing Logan.

"Everything is fine." Meri smiled when Logan pointed at a few geese flying overhead. He dropped into the grass and spread out on his back to watch the birds navigate above him. "How's the Cortez case going?"

Marta scrunched her nose and twisted her full lips. "I've spent the last two nights sitting outside a nasty motel on the east side of town. I've seen plenty of questionable things, but I haven't seen her husband once."

"Instead of waiting for him to show, go to his office and follow him."

"Lynn's a bit worried about me following someone. She thinks I need more practice first."

Meri was actually relieved to hear that. She was still on the fence about Marta taking the case at all.

"I'll teach you some things when this is done."

Marta's eyes lit up. "That'd be great, Meri. Thank you."

"You're welcome. I appreciate you playing with him. He needed it."

"He's a good kid."

"He really is. Bring him in when you get tired, okay?"

"Will do," Marta said before daring Logan to beat her to the tree line.

He sprang to his feet as if he hadn't been running endlessly for the last hour or so. Yeah, he definitely needed to burn off some energy. Meri was glad they'd found a nice, quiet place for him to do that.

She was even more glad, she realized, that she was there to share this place with Troy. Looking out the window, she saw him still watching over the yard. Watching her.

Like a beacon guiding her home, she headed straight for him.

Troy couldn't take his eyes off Meri as she walked back inside and right to him. He opened his arms, and she collapsed against his chest. He hugged her close and kissed the top of her head. There would never come a time that he wouldn't want to hold this woman like this. The soft scent of lavender drifted up from her hair and filled his entire being. He could breathe her in forever, but the miserable-sounding sigh that emanated from her distracted him.

"Are you okay?" he asked.

"I love you," she said softly. "But I'd choose to save Logan over you. You know that, right?"

A short laugh rumbled through his chest. "I never doubted that."

"And you'd save Logan over me." She leaned her head back to look into his eyes. "Right?"

"Yes. Without hesitation."

Meri nodded like she believed him, but even so, she said, "If you ever think for a moment—"

He tugged her a bit closer to him to stop her from sounding so uncertain. "If anyone around here takes a bullet, it will be you," he said lightly, but then he let the shadow of a smile fall from his lips. "The kid comes first, Meri. Always."

"Always," she agreed and then leaned into him again.

Ever since he had kissed her the night before, the urge to touch her hadn't ceased. He didn't know if it ever would. Simply being close to her lit the darkness that had hovered over him for far too long. He let out a long slow breath and hugged Meri even closer.

"Lynn's worried you'll choose me over Logan," he said.

Meri leaned into him and wrapped her arms around his waist. "No. She's worried I'll choose you over Prestige when you go home."

Troy hadn't taken the time to think about what would happen when all of this ended and he could go back to New York. *If* he could go back to New York. Yes, he'd acted in his capacity as a bodyguard when he'd taken Logan, but the agency may not agree with him on that. They could very well see him as a child abductor. They could fire him and send him to jail.

If that happened, the likelihood would be that they'd try to drag Meri and her team to jail as co-conspirators in Logan's abduction. He wished he had considered that before he dragged her and her colleague into this mess.

"Stop," Meri whispered. Leaning her head back, she looked up at him. "None of this is your fault."

"How do you—"

"Because I know how that pea brain of yours works." Though she'd criticized the size of his brain, she'd done so with a teasing grin. "We knew what we were getting into. We did it anyway." Pulling away from him, she started for the kitchen. "Joanie brought way more food than I think we'll need, but that should save us from having to make any trips into town for a few days."

"That's good," Troy said.

"Does Logan like lasagna?" she asked as she got a mug from a cabinet.

"I think so." Leaning on the counter, he watched as she filled a mug with the strong brew.

Though she presented herself with hard edges and a granite exterior, her movements were amazingly graceful, even when making a cup of coffee. Once again, he realized how much he had longed to be able to look at her so openly. Now that he no longer had to keep his infatuation with her secret, he couldn't stop himself from taking in everything about her.

Her lips curved into a smirk as she dumped far too much sugar into her coffee. "What?"

"You're beautiful," he said as she sweetened her drink.

A soft laugh was all the acknowledgment she made of his compliment. That didn't surprise him. She never had been the type that needed validation from him or anyone else.

"Now that we are somewhat settled," she said, "we need to set up space to review the case. We should do that while the team is here to distract Logan. I hope to hell you're wrong about Randall," she added, stirring her coffee as she stared at him, obviously waiting for him to reassure her.

While Troy hoped his longtime colleague wasn't responsible for the Bantams' murders, he wasn't confident enough to voice his hopes.

"Let's use the loft," he said. "It's best to keep the investigation away from Logan. I don't want to upset him. I'll grab my folder and see you up there."

By the time he reached the top of the stairs, Meri was logged in to the computer.

"I'm printing off what Casey found on Randall's bank accounts. Nothing is standing out. It looks like he took out a loan against his retirement to pay for the car."

Though she sounded relieved, Troy's suspicions didn't ease. Snagging the roll of Scotch tape off the desk, he started taping his notes to the wall. This was the same setup they used at Lochlin Private Security. A mass of evidence taped to the walls might confuse a lot of people, but it worked for him and Meri.

Hearing Logan squeal, Troy peered out the big windows. His heart had seized for a moment, but he was able to relax and smile as he watched Logan laugh when Marta wrapped him in a big bear hug and spun him around. The two of them seemed to have tapped into some kind of endless energy supply, and he was thankful to Marta for that.

He still hadn't recovered from being the only person responsible for Logan's safety for days on end. He'd catch up on his sleep soon, he suspected, but right now, he didn't have it in him to be a playmate to the boy.

"Look at that guy run," Troy said after Logan broke free from Marta's arms and darted across the grass again.

"He could win a race or two, huh?" Meri gathered papers off the printer. She didn't look at him, but she apparently saw him from the corner of her eye. That sexy grin of hers pulled at her mouth as she skimmed over the papers in her hand. "I can feel you staring at me," she said, several pounding heartbeats later.

"Want me to stop?"

Turning to face him, she held his gaze and took a big, deep breath. As she let it out, she crooked her finger, silently insisting he come to her. He crossed the room in a few big steps and pulled the papers from her hand. Tossing them onto the desk, he wrapped his arm around her waist and yanked her against him.

Her smile spread as he lifted her feet off the floor enough to carry her out of view of the windows. If anyone looked up, they wouldn't be able to peer in and see what was happening in the loft.

"Oh, Troy. You are so suave," she teased as he eased her feet back to the carpet.

"You have no idea." He covered her mouth with his and cupped the back of her head, holding her against him.

The day before, he had longed to deepen their kisses, but Logan had woken from his nap and interrupted the moment. The little guy was outside now, under the protective eyes of the Prestige team. There would be no interruptions this time.

Meri opened her mouth enough to slide her tongue over his lips. Her movement encouraged him to do the same. She tasted of the sweet coffee she'd been sipping. Somehow that fit her so perfectly—sweet, bold. Strong.

Just like the first time they kissed, over a year ago, everything faded away. Her heat enveloped him, and her taste consumed him. Being with her like this felt so right, like every choice he'd ever made—good and bad—was leading to this moment. He'd realized long ago that he was in love with her but feeling her arms around him made his entire body ache. This was more than love; this was the other half of his soul finally coming home.

She tilted her head, pulling from his kiss, then nipped her teeth along his jaw. Some primal sound—a deep guttural growl—formed in his throat as she moved her assault to his neck. His body sprang to life at the feel of her pressing hers against him.

She moaned and sank her bite lightly into the flesh on his neck, and Troy very nearly lost what little sense he was able to hold on to around this woman. He clenched her shirt into his fists to stop himself from tearing her clothes from her body right there.

"You're killing me," he said in a tense whisper.

"Good," she replied with that damned teasing voice of hers.

He was debating pushing her to the floor and having sex with her right there in the loft and probably would have if the screen door hadn't slammed. The chattering of voices interrupted their heated exchange, and they both cursed.

Troy stepped back as Meri tugged her shirt down. The flush on her face and the way her hair was a mess from his hold on the strands stoked the fire that was already threatening to consume him. She looked like a goddamn goddess standing before him, and all he wanted was to go back to worshiping her.

Stroking his hand over her head, he did his best to fix the mess he'd made. "You wait until we're alone," he threatened barely above a whisper.

She gave him that sexy smile of hers. "As I was saying before I was so *rudely* interrupted," she said, "the money for Randall's new car is legit. He borrowed against his retirement. That doesn't mean, however, that he wasn't paid off by someone. He's smart. He knows how to cover his tracks. He very well could have borrowed that money knowing he had funds in an offshore account for his golden years."

She held the report out to him and focused on the research on his teammates that he'd taped to the wall. Suddenly she froze and squinted at something. Leaning closer, she stared, analyzing an image.

Troy skimmed the photo, trying to decipher what had caught her eye. "Meri?"

"Who is that?" she asked, pointing at a picture of Randall's new girlfriend.

"That's the woman I was telling you about. The woman he started dating right after the Bantams went into hiding. I don't have much on her yet. I was working on that when they were murdered and we had to run."

She leaned even closer to the photo of Randall and the brunette he'd been schmoozing with without anyone else's knowledge.—at least not until Troy had started following his teammates. "That sneaky motherfucker," she said through ground teeth.

"What is it?"

"That," she stated, poking her pointer finger at the woman's image, "is Ana Cortez. She hired Prestige the very day that you appeared in my living room. That's the case I handed off to Marta."

"Son of a bitch," he breathed. "He knew I would come to you. He sent her in to watch you."

She nodded. "Which means he probably knows, or at least suspects, that we're using my team to help you."

"Did she request you work her case?"

"No. That was luck on her part. However, passing her off to Marta had to have sent up a flag for Randall. If he didn't know you were here, he likely has figured it out. He's going to be watching all of them, waiting for them to lead him to Logan." She frowned and rolled her head back. "Damn it."

"We knew this could happen. We've been careful."

"Yes, but confirming that he's here changes things. We have to tell the team to stay away. They could lead him right to us."

"There goes our backup," Troy muttered. "We should run. Hit the road like we initially planned."

"No." Meri pressed her lips together as she shook her head. "He doesn't know we're on to her. We can use that to our advantage."

"How so?"

"We're going to follow her," she said. "She'll lead us to Randall eventually."

"And then what?"

She smirked. "And then I'll break every bone in his fucking body, one by one, until he confesses to being a sellout and putting that kid's life in danger."

Troy would have laughed had he thought for a moment she was joking. "Well. The first part of your plan is okay. I think we need to work on the rest of it."

She pouted slightly, and he couldn't help himself. He leaned in and kissed her.

"One bone," he conceded. "You can break one bone."

"Fine. As long as it's a big one. Like his skull."

[7]

Meri glanced at her phone and tried to hide her frustration at the lack of communication she'd gotten from Prestige.

The team had quickly surmised Ana Cortez's philandering husband didn't exist. The sob story had been a ruse to get her close to Meri and, presumably, to Troy and Logan. After they worked out their plan, Marta had called the woman in to "give an update" on the investigation into Ana's so-called cheating spouse. Marta was going to ask lots of questions and make sure Ana drank from a cup to get her prints. In the meantime, Lynn and Casey prepared to follow Ana to wherever she was staying.

Once Ana left the office, Trista was tasked with taking the cup to Justin, Lynn's cop boyfriend, to see if he could identify her through her fingerprints. *If* they were able to get Ana's real name, Trista and Marta would gather as much information on the woman as they could find. Meri suspected they wouldn't find much even if they were able to identify her. Randall was as capable as Meri and Troy at erasing old identities and creating new ones.

Ana Cortez was a fake, and the Prestige team was going to have a hell of a time getting to the truth about her.

"Come on," Meri muttered under her breath as her irritation grew. She was itching to confront Randall, but she couldn't do that until Ana led the way to the backstabbing bastard.

"Patience, sweetheart," Troy said as he pulled the lasagna from the oven.

She instantly imagined those words growled into her ear as he pinned her to the bed, and she practically melted into a puddle at his feet.

All the times she'd dreamed of being with him like that... But she hadn't anticipated his touch burning into her soul the way it had. She could still feel his hands on her. His mouth teasing her. His breath heating her.

They'd wasted too much time pretending they hadn't wanted each other. She was glad they didn't have to lie about that any longer. Leaning forward, she rested her forearms on the counter and smiled as she watched him reach for plates from the cabinet next to her. Tilting her head, she took a moment to admire the snug fit of his jeans.

"I was thinking about earlier."

He moaned a sound that vibrated from his chest all the way to her ears. "We *will* find time to finish that," he promised.

Her cheeks warmed. She really was blushing now. "Yes, we will."

Troy looked over his shoulder and winked as he set the

plates down. "Hey, Logan. Go wash up, please. Dinner's ready."

Meri pushed herself to stand upright as Logan darted toward the bathroom. "Must be hungry," she said. "He's probably running on empty after all that time playing with Marta." She giggled when Troy pulled her against him and put her hand to his chest as he gave her a quick, hard kiss. "I was talking."

"There are better ways to spend those rare moments we are alone."

Another little laugh left her, and she wanted to roll her eyes at herself. She wasn't a gushy, giggly schoolgirl. Yet here she was acting like one. Trista would be offended—that was usually her role.

As Logan's heavy footfalls started again, Meri stepped away from Troy and set about readying the table for dinner.

"Did you even have time to get your hands wet?" she asked as Logan ran into the room.

He grinned mischievously. "Yup."

She suspected that was all he had time for but didn't call him out for not using soap. He'd had a rough few weeks. Did she really care if he didn't wash his hands properly?

After handing him three forks to put on the table, she poured him a glass of milk while Troy finished serving. They sat around the table, and she felt that same strange sense of peace wash over her that she'd felt when Troy resurfaced in her life.

They were in danger. All of them, but mostly this innocent little boy. But as they sat there, listening to him excitedly ramble about playing with Marta and how much he wanted to explore the woods around the house, Meri felt more herself than she had in over a year. She and Troy used to sneak away for quiet dinners all the time, but this was hardly sneaking and definitely not quiet. Yet it brought about that same kind of belonging she'd always felt when it was only the two of them.

Logan barely stopped talking, even when he had food in his mouth, and Troy repeatedly reminded him of his manners. He'd stop talking, swallow hard, then start up again. They had told him they planned to stay there until he could *go back*, being careful not to say home or to see his parents, and that had perked him up. He'd settled in quickly, but Meri hadn't expected to see this chatterbox side of him.

At one point, she widened her eyes and looked at Troy as if to verify he was seeing the same thing she was. He laughed softly and nodded. He had understood her question via that strange unspoken communication they'd always shared.

"Don't get him started on race cars," Troy whispered.

Logan didn't hear the warning, or at least he didn't respond to it. He was too busy telling Meri and Troy that Joanie said she would take him out in the canoe soon. Since he wasn't a good swimmer, he added, she was going to buy him a life jacket first.

Meri was so caught up in constant conversation that she didn't even think to check her phone until they had all cleared their plates and Logan was trying to talk his way out of taking a shower. As he was listing off reasons, including that he'd taken a shower the night before, her phone rang, and she pushed herself from the table to answer the call.

"Hey," Troy said, looking at Logan, "go get your pajamas on."

"No shower?" Logan asked.

"No. But brush your teeth and grab a book. I'll be there in a few."

His excitement faded. "It's not bedtime yet."

Troy pointed toward the hallway. "Go."

Logan pouted as he headed for his bedroom.

Meri put her phone on speaker as Troy joined her at the counter.

"Hey," she said. "We're here. What's up?"

"I think he's been watching you for a while," Lynn said through the phone. "They are staying in a house two blocks from yours. I doubt that is a coincidence."

"No, it's not. That asshole," Meri muttered under her breath.

"Did he have any idea how to find you?" Lynn asked. "Were you ever in contact with him?"

"No."

Troy ran his hand over his hair, clearly frustrated. "It took me almost a year to figure out where you'd gone. He couldn't have done it in two weeks."

"Were you using every resource available to you?" Meri asked.

"No," he said flatly.

She shrugged, convinced that explained how Randall had found her faster. "The higher-ups were able to access other agencies and sort through all the paperwork it took to change my name and relocate. You didn't have the clearance to do that. *They* did. They sent him. They're here."

"Why would Lochlin use Randall's girlfriend to gather intel?"

"It looks like it's just the two of them," Lynn said, interrupting their debate. "I'm not seeing any signs that they have backup. Casey's driving around the neighborhood to see if she can spot anyone else watching the house. We'll take turns keeping an eye on the house. Honestly, though, I don't think the entirety of Lochlin is in on this. This doesn't feel like an organized operation. Is there anyone you can call to see if Randall is on the run too?"

Meri and Troy looked at each other, silently questioning the other. Finally, Meri said, "We'll see what we can find out."

"Thanks, Lynn," Troy added.

"I'll let you know if either of them leaves."

"Any word on the Bantams' nanny?" Meri asked.

"Yeah, she's working for a family in Manhattan now. Casey's digging deeper, but I don't think there's anything more there than Richard Bantam screwing the help."

"Damn it," Meri muttered. "Thanks for checking."

"I'll keep you posted." Lynn ended the call.

Meri tossed her phone down. "You're right. Lochlin would never use a civilian. Maybe Ana is a security professional for another company."

Troy shook his head. "No. I watched her long enough to know she's not trained."

"If he is on the run..." She let her words fade, hating what that implied. Being on the run meant he was guilty of something, because he sure as hell wasn't sneaking around town to protect Logan. "Damn it. He's always been a good guard. A strong guard. Why would he—"

"Money, Meri. The same reason the majority of the people in the world do anything. He was bought and paid for by someone."

"His being here can only mean one thing."

"He's after Logan."

She nodded as the sense of concern for the boy deepened. Not that she hadn't been concerned before, but now the threat was real. Palpable. Close. And smart. She could attest to how incredibly capable Randall Gillion was. If he was after Logan, she and Troy were up against a formidable opponent.

And not knowing what Ana Cortez—or whatever her real name was—brought to the table made Meri even more uneasy. Meri could think like Randall—they'd worked together for years—but she didn't know a damn thing about the woman at his side. Or how dangerous she could be.

Troy shook his head and leaned against the counter. "As soon as Prestige confirms no one is watching him, we should kick the fucking door in."

"We don't have that authority."

He shrugged. "I haven't been officially fired. I'm still protecting a client."

"You haven't checked in with the director *to* get officially fired."

He smirked. "That's just a technicality, boss."

She laughed. "Oh, I forgot what a handful you can be."

Troy dipped his head down and smiled as innocently as a cherub. "I'm happy to remind you."

Ignoring his double entendre, she said, "As much as I'd love to barge in there, we have to be smart about this. He could be armed. This could be a trap to lure you in. There could be a hundred ways this goes down that we haven't considered. We have to be careful." She glanced toward the hallway, making sure they were still alone, before she whispered, "The last thing we want is for Logan to end up back in the hands of someone who *may* have killed his parents."

Troy lifted his dark brows as he stared at her. "Tell me you aren't still doubting Randall's involvement. This all but proves—"

"That he's on the run. Doesn't mean he's the one who killed them. But..." She looked toward the hall again. "We can't do anything to put him in more danger than he already is."

"You should take him and disappear." Troy lost the tense edge to his tone. He was serious. "Don't tell anyone, even me, where you take him."

"I don't know if he can take going on the run again, Troy. Did you see how happy he was to be in a normal setting? He needs some stability before we do permanent damage to him."

"More permanent than getting him killed? He'll have to suck it up. It's the smartest thing to do, Meri."

"Is it?" she asked. "We have a small army here with Prestige. Maybe the smartest thing is to stand our ground. We should flush him out and put an end to this on our terms."

"I can't put your team in danger."

"They agreed to help us despite the danger."

"They don't understand—"

"They do," she insisted. "They know who is after him and why, and they chose to put themselves between him and the danger chasing him anyway. The women I work with aren't pushovers, Troy. They're tough. They can take this." Putting her hand to his cheek, she sighed. "We're here to help you keep him safe. *All* of us. There is no better place to have a showdown than here, with my team beside us."

He didn't voice his relief, but she could see it in his eyes. Pulling her to him, he rested his hands on her waist.

"I love you," he whispered.

She smiled. "I love you."

He threaded his fingers into her hair and kissed her lightly. The moment their lips touched, Logan called out to Troy that he was ready for his bedtime story.

Troy exhaled loudly. "How do parents ever find time to be together?"

Meri laughed. "I have no idea. Go," she said. "I'll clean up."

He pressed a kiss to her forehead before disappearing down the hallway.

As soon as she was done cleaning the kitchen, she followed his voice to the tiny bedroom. They were huddled on the bed, reading together. She guessed that one book was all they could add to their backpacks while on the run. She made a mental note to have one of the women at her office pick up a few more for him.

Though she wanted Prestige to keep their distance to make certain they couldn't be followed, they'd have to bring groceries eventually. They'd run out of milk and fresh produce at some point. When those needed to be replenished, a few new books could be added to the shopping list.

Logan noticed her watching from the door and waved her over. She sat on the side of the bed and listened as Troy expertly read about a cool cat and his adventures. Logan giggled at the voices Troy was making, and Meri had to smile.

When the story ended, Meri gently said, "Night, buddy."

"Night, Meri."

Troy closed the book and started to stand, but Logan grabbed him.

His eyes grew wide. "You can't *both* leave. Somebody has to stay with me in case the bad guys come."

The fear in his voice made Meri's chest ache. She'd said to Troy earlier that she didn't want to cause any permanent damage to the kid, but in that moment, she realized it was probably too late.

Troy eased back onto the bed. "I'll stay."

Logan relaxed as he fell back against his pillows. Though he had insisted it wasn't bedtime, and it really wasn't yet, the exhaustion in his eyes was evident. Between the weeks on the run and an afternoon spent playing in the fresh air, he was more tired than he was willing to admit. She guessed it wouldn't take more than fifteen minutes for him to slip into a deep sleep.

"I'll be upstairs," she said to Troy. He nodded as Logan curled up against him. Whoever Logan ended up with when this was over was going to have a hell of a time breaking him of his need to have someone stay with him at almost all times. They were going to have a hell of a time helping him with *a lot* of things. Including coping with the loss of his parents.

A dark cloud formed in the back of her mind as she thought about all the struggles Logan was going to have when this was over. She turned his overhead light out as she left the room, then crossed the hall and turned on the bathroom light to offer some illumination in the hallway. Shaking off the sense of worry over Logan's future, she walked upstairs to check the monitors, reminding herself they had to get him out of this mess before his recovery could become a real concern.

Troy slowed his stride as he entered the loft and spied Meri staring at the wall of evidence they'd put up earlier. His mind strayed to other things, though. Like pinning her against the wall and nipping at her neck as she ground her ass against him.

She glanced over but didn't hold his gaze for more than a few seconds. "We should confront him."

"Huh?" he asked, genuinely confused. He'd been so lost in thought that he hadn't fully understood what she'd said.

"Randall. We should call Ana and demand she put him on the phone so we can schedule a meeting."

"That could be dangerous."

"It could also put an end to this."

"I was considering calling Director Bruce to let him know I'm in hiding with the kid and I found out Randall is closing in on us. See what he has to say."

She eyed him. "Even with burner phones, that's pretty risky."

"I'll keep the call short. I need to get a feel for what's happening on their end. I think we should hold off on tipping our hand to Randall. Let me reach out first."

Nodding, she looked over the printouts again. "How do you think Logan is doing? Really?"

Troy blew out his breath slowly. "I don't know, Meri. Other than my nieces and nephews, I don't have much experience with kids. None of them have ever been through anything like this, so I don't really know how to read his reactions. I tried to make this a big adventure, but he knows something is wrong. He's obviously afraid to be alone. I don't know if that's because I've been pounding it into his head that he can't trust anyone but me or if he was exposed to what happened to his parents."

"Has he asked to speak to them?"

He shook his head. "He knows. He has to know."

She agreed with a slight nod. "What's going to happen to him?"

Troy had tried not to think about that too much. He knew better than to bond with a witness, but that was next to impossible when that witness was a terrified kid.

"Once it's safe for him, they'll find a home. A relative or a family capable of helping him."

She looked sad, and Troy understood. The thought of Logan being put into the system made him sad too, but there wasn't much they could do about that. Lochlin Private Security was ultimately responsible for his well-being. Once Troy turned him back over to the agency, they would determine what would happen to him.

Even though Troy didn't know who to trust on his team,

he hoped Lochlin would do what was best for Logan. They'd make sure that he was cared for and had the professional help he needed to come to terms with losing his parents.

"Everything good out there?" He nodded toward the monitors.

"Yup. Nice and quiet."

"Good."

Gently grabbing her arm, he pulled her against his chest. She leaned into him, wrapping her arms around his waist as he tightened his around her shoulders.

He held her close for several long seconds before whispering, "Can we shelve all this for about an hour or so?"

Lifting her head, she eyed him as her lips twitched into a slight grin. "That would be wonderful."

He kissed her—a real kiss without interruption—taking his time to meld his mouth to hers and allow himself to soak up the feel of her. She started to deepen the kiss, to amp up the passion, but Troy put his hands to her face. The exchange they'd had earlier was hot and frenzied and threatened to consume them. Now he wanted to take a few moments to enjoy and appreciate tasting her.

Moving his lips to her jaw, he placed soft kisses along it and then down her throat.

She sighed, breathed his name, and tightened her hands in his hair. "You're trouble, aren't you?"

"I hope so," he said with a smile. If he hadn't known before, he did then. He loved her. With every bit of his soul, he loved this woman.

[8]

The moment Ana Cortez walked into the Prestige conference room, Meri slammed the door behind her before Marta could follow her in. Not that Marta was going to. She had lured Ana to the office. Meri was going to do the rest.

Though Troy had been hesitant to confront Randall, Meri's gut told her that was the right thing to do. Troy had been on edge too long. He wasn't seeing the most logical steps right now. He was so concerned with keeping Logan safe that he wasn't looking for a way out. She was. And she knew this was it.

She wouldn't tell Troy about this unless she felt that she'd made progress. Not to be sneaky but because he had enough on his mind. If she could end this without adding to his stress, that would benefit them all.

As a team leader, she'd often had to make calls that went against what other members of her team felt was the best option. She was right most of the time. And she was convinced she was right this time.

Confronting Randall, calling him out, was going to knock him off balance and give them the upper hand. Having his *friend* in her custody wasn't a bad deal either. If Randall tried to stonewall Meri, she wasn't above using a few nonlethal moves to get a few painful cries from the woman to loosen Randall's tongue.

If that didn't work, Ana would turn on him for not coming to her defense. Either way, Meri was going to get some answers. She hoped it didn't come to hurting this weakling of a woman, but she would do what she had to.

The woman jolted and turned around. Her eyes grew wide, but she tried to hide it with a light laugh.

"Meri. You startled me," she said, putting her hand to her chest.

Meri didn't smile in return. She held Ana's gaze as she made a deliberate show of locking the conference room door. Subtle but intimidating. If Ana were a professional, she wouldn't be shaken, but as Ana watched, her face paled.

She stuttered and then forced her smile back into place. "Marta told me you were ill. I'm glad to see you're feeling better."

Leaning against the door, Meri crossed her arms and gave Ana her hardest stare. Ana's gaze darted from Meri's face to the gun in full view on Meri's hip to the locked door, then back to Meri's stone-cold eyes. Other than the sound of Ana's audible swallow, heavy silence filled the room.

The silent showdown was obviously making this little twit uncomfortable. Good. Let her squirm. And squirm Ana did. Meri took resting bitch face to an epic level. When she leveled her stare and clenched her jaw, grown men would break before her. Ana didn't stand a chance.

If Randall had been any kind of boyfriend, he wouldn't have put Ana in this position. If he'd been any kind of leader, he would have prepped her for Meri's signature move—the ultimate death stare. This proved that he didn't have what it took to be the team leader that he'd always tried to be. This is why Meri was promoted over him and why Troy thought he might be resentful enough to sell out a Lochlin Private Security family.

"I-I-I..."

"You what, *Ana*?" Meri emphasized the woman's name because she was certain it was as fake as the woman's story.

She swallowed again.

Pushing herself from the door, Meri took one big step to close the distance between them. Nose-to-nose, she continued to stare.

"Call him."

Ana didn't move, but she made a pathetic whimpering sound.

"Call him," Meri said again. "Now."

The woman's hands trembled as she fumbled with her purse. She had failed the test. Troy was right. "Ana Cortez" definitely hadn't been professionally trained. She was too timid to have ever faced real danger. Meri almost felt bad for her.

Randall liked to play games to get laid. Meri had warned him a thousand times that he was going to lead the wrong woman on and get himself in real trouble. He likely didn't suspect the trouble would be Meri using his foolhardy lover to get to him.

As soon as Ana dialed and started to put the phone to her ear, Meri snatched it from her hand. She listened to the ringing, still pinning Ana in place with her gaze.

"Hey," a man answered, and Meri immediately recognized his voice. "What's going on?"

"Why don't you tell me, Randall?" Meri asked.

He was silent, but only for a moment. "Took you long enough," he said. "You losing your touch, Meri?"

She gently pushed Ana into a chair. "What are you doing here?"

"I came to protect Logan Bantam. And you."

"Somehow I doubt that."

"I didn't snuff out that family," Randall insisted. "But I know how it looks."

Meri stepped back but kept her eyes on Ana, not trusting her any more than she trusted the man on the phone.

"Oh, yeah. How's that?"

"The money I've been spending. Makes it look like I've been paid off."

"Yeah. It does."

He sighed. "Come on, Meri. You know me better than that."

"Do I?"

"I'd hope so. You got a gun on my girl?"

"Not yet, but I'm not above shooting her to get to the bottom of this."

Ana let out a soft cry, and her lip trembled. "Randall?" she called.

Meri lifted her hand to hush her.

"Ask her what her name is. Her real name."

Cocking her head, Meri stared at the woman. "What's your real name?"

"Ana...Gillion. I'm Randall's wife."

Meri didn't like being surprised. But she was.

"We got married three months ago," Randall explained. "I can afford to buy nicer things now. We have a pretty good second income."

"So you got married and didn't tell anyone?"

"I wanted to protect her. From *him*, Meri."

"Who?"

His sigh was dramatic. "Troy."

She felt a chill roll down her spine. "I don't—"

"He's been obsessed with you for years. We all knew it. It was kind of cute for a while, you know. New guy crushing on our badass boss. But then you guys started hanging out off the clock, and it became annoying how smitten he was. Then you left, and his obsession got scary. He damn near lost his mind when the director told us that you quit. We all protested when Troy was put as our new team lead. Nobody who gets that infatuated with someone should be making decisions for a team. The director passed it off as sour grapes, but Hank and I knew there was something wrong with him."

Meri registered the mention of her other Lochlin Private Security teammate. She considered reaching out to him to get his take on what Randall was telling her.

Though she was having a hard time seeing this side of Troy, she also couldn't deny that she'd known long before leaving the team that he had feelings for her. Maybe they ran deeper—and more dangerous—than she'd realized.

"He was checking our phone records," Randall said. "He was following us to see if we met up with you. Nobody had talked to you, but he didn't believe it. I got worried about his behavior, and I followed him one night. He sat outside your mother's house for hours, Meri. *Hours.* Just watching."

Another rush of anxiety rolled over her at the thought of Troy or anyone else watching her mom. The hazard of working a job like hers was that family could be pulled into the crosshairs if someone felt vengeful. She taught her team to never talk about their personal lives with clients, but she'd never told them to keep that same distance from their colleagues.

Randall continued, "That was the last straw. I went to Director Bruce and filed a complaint. He did an official inquiry. He agreed Troy was overstepping and threatened to have him suspended if he didn't stop looking for you. He said it was abuse of resources, but the truth was his actions were bordering on stalking. Troy knows it was me. He knows I turned him in. That's why he's setting me up to take the fall for what he's done."

"Why the hell would he do that?"

"To get to *you*," Randall stressed. "Are you listening to me?"

She hardened her gaze at Ana simply because Randall wasn't there for her to glare at. "Yes, but how do those two things connect?"

"He finally found you. That's the only thing that makes sense."

"None of this makes sense, Randall," she said, letting far more anger fill her tone than she'd intended.

"He found you, and he did what he had to do to justify going to you. He killed that family and took the kid so he'd have a reason to show up at your door."

A knife went through her gut, and she shook her head. "Bullshit. Troy didn't kill anybody."

"It didn't even take him ten minutes to show once he got the call that something had happened. The safe house was over twenty minutes from the office and thirty minutes from Troy's apartment. No way he was in the neighborhood. He was close because he'd killed them."

"No, he knew something was going to happen."

"All he talked about until the director put a stop to it was how he was going to find you and bring you back. He was going to bring you back to the team, and things were going to go back to normal. He was fixated on that, Meri."

"Look," she said, refusing to believe him, "the reason I left was because—"

"Sarah caught you and Troy together and took off right before she got killed."

This time the audible swallow came from Meri. "He told you that?"

"No. Sarah called me after Troy told her that he was going to put in for a transfer. I was the only other person who knew about what was going on with them."

Meri opened her mouth, but no words would form. *Going on with them?*

"I saw her making googly eyes at him one day and warned her to knock it off," Randall explained. "I told her romancing a teammate was against policy, and even if he would violate that, he only had eyes for you. She told me it was too late. He was tired of the way you always blew him off and had hooked up with her. They were lovers, Meri."

The air whooshed out of Meri's lungs like she'd been sucker-punched. "That's not true."

"Are you sure about that?"

She didn't answer. She didn't know how.

Randall sighed again. "She called me, screaming and crying after she caught you two together. She was upset because she'd caught her boyfriend cheating on her."

"None of what you are saying adds up, Randall. Troy killed that family because he was obsessed with finding me? No. I don't believe you."

"Goddamn it, Meri. You're smarter than this. He needed a way to lure you in. If he'd just shown up at your door, you could have slammed it in his face, but he knew you couldn't turn away a client. Especially a kid."

Meri shook her head even though Randall couldn't see her through the phone.

"I was keeping an eye on Troy. I shadowed his computer for a long time. I had all the same information he did, and I was doing my own research. When the kid disappeared, they put us all on leave while they straightened out this mess. I knew exactly where Troy was going, so I came here too. Only difference is that I am here to help you. And to protect Logan from harm."

"*Really?*" she asked with sarcastic disbelief.

"Look." He let out a heavy sigh. "I'm on leave, but I'm still a bodyguard. I'm still working for Lochlin. That kid is in danger. Do you really think Troy went to these lengths to get his hands on you to share you with a kid? He'll off him as soon as he thinks he has you locked in, and he'll make it look like a hit. Just like he did with his parents. He is using Logan to manipulate you. Once he doesn't need him anymore, that kid is dead."

Meri felt sick to her stomach. "Randall—"

"I sent Ana to hire you. To get you alone so I could reach out to you. I was hoping to get to you before Troy did, but as soon as you handed her case off, I knew it was too late. I was watching your house, but you must have slipped by me. I lost track of you, but I knew at some point you were going to figure out her case was fake and find your way to me."

She swallowed as she looked at the woman still trembling in front of her.

"He's dangerous, Meri," Randall told her. "If you don't believe me, that's fine. Don't. But reach out to the director and get that kid back into protective custody. Don't put his life in danger because you aren't thinking clearly. Don't let Troy use that little boy to get to you."

Meri grabbed one of the pads of sticky notes and a pen from a stack on the table. "What's Hank's number?" When Randall rambled it off, she jotted the number down. "And yours?" She added it to the paper. "I'll call you."

"Meri—" Randall started.

"I'll call you." She ended the call and handed the phone back to Ana.

"He's been really worried about you," Ana said in a soft voice. "Not just the boy, but you. You should know that. He's a good guy. Randall, I mean. He's been so worried."

Meri jerked her head toward the door. "Leave. And don't you say a word about this to anyone. Understand?"

She nodded and rushed from the conference room straight to the front door.

Meri watched her leave before marching into Lynn's office. "We may have a problem," she stated as acid started to churn in her stomach.

Troy's heart sank to his stomach when he heard gravel crunching in the driveway. As he gripped his gun, he looked to where Logan was examining rocks near the water. Releasing the snap on his holster, he was ready to draw his weapon, but he immediately recognized Lynn's sedan. She was bringing Meri back to him.

Though the Prestige team had provided them with a cheap car, he insisted the car stay there in case something happened. Instead of Meri driving herself to the office for a meeting, Lynn picked her up. She said she would have missed the meeting, but it was crucial she be there to help resolve an issue with one of her teammates.

That was definitely the downside of having a team. One of them was always willing to start trouble. At some point, Troy was going to have to come clean with the full story on why he was hesitant for her to contact Randall, but he was hoping it wouldn't come to that. If he could get this mess sorted out first, she'd never believe what Randall told her anyway.

Re-snapping his holster, he pulled his flannel shirt over

the gun and smiled as Meri climbed from the car. He was so focused on her walking to him that he didn't even notice Marta getting out of the back seat until Logan called out to her.

She smiled big and held up her hand to get his high-five. "What are you up to, little dude?" she asked.

"Come look at these rocks. They are *so* cool."

Troy laughed as Logan pulled her toward the rocky little beach. "You are in it now," he warned.

She smiled. "I don't mind."

"Hey, you," Meri said to Troy as she stopped in front of him.

Her voice was stiff and cold.

He was about to ask her if something was wrong, but then Lynn warned Marta if she got her shoes muddy, she was walking back to the office.

He brushed off Meri's cool greeting as her being a bit aloof in front of her boss. Even though Meri and Troy had known each other a long time, he supposed it wasn't good for her boss to know they'd become lovers the night before. And that morning.

He sighed, recalling how she'd come to relieve him from watching the monitors in the wee hours. And how they'd taken advantage of the quiet house and the privacy of the loft once again before he'd gotten a few hours of rest while she took over the role of protector. He had to draw a long deep breath to stop himself from pulling her to him. Everything in him wanted to kiss her until she couldn't breathe.

Later, he reminded himself.

She smiled a secret smile as she walked by him and

subtly nodded toward the house. He glanced at Lynn and Marta, keeping an eye on Logan before following Meri. Troy had to chuckle at his reaction. Though there would be no lovemaking in the next few stolen moments, he was definitely going to sneak in a few heated kisses. He practically started salivating like Pavlov's dog, eager for his treat, as he followed Meri into the house.

Once inside, they both peered out the window before Meri grabbed his hand and pulled him toward the hallway. The moment they stepped into the master bedroom, he held her against him for an open-mouthed kiss.

She didn't resist, but she didn't give in either. Something was off.

The unbridled passion they'd shared multiple times in the last few days was lacking. Not lacking. It was gone. Leaning back, he eyed her, but she diverted her gaze, focusing on where she pressed her hands to his chest, and then gave him a gentle shove.

"Get undressed," she whispered, as she'd done the night before.

He laughed softly. "We can't... Lynn and Marta are right outside."

She smiled. "I know."

Troy laughed softly. "You're crazy," he muttered. Even so, he wasn't about to deny either of them a moment together. He cupped her face and put a hard kiss to her lips before moving to the nightstand and removing his gun from the holster and his knife from his pocket. He started working on the buttons of his shirt as he turned.

Immediately his smile fell.

She'd taken her gun from her holster too, but she hadn't set it aside. She'd aimed her Glock at him from across the room.

He lifted his hands. "Whoa. What are you doing?"

"Step away from your weapons, Troy."

"Meri—"

"Step away from your weapons."

He took two big steps toward her.

"Stop right there," she ordered.

He did. He also kept his hands up, not wanting her to mistake any movement he made as a threat. "What the fuck is going on?"

The hurt in her eyes was obvious. Yet there she was, loaded weapon in hand.

"I need you to tell me the truth," she said.

"About what?"

"Everything, Troy. From the time I left New York until the time you showed up in my house. Tell me everything."

He stared at her. Tried to read her. Finally, he realized what had changed. "You confronted Randall. The issue you needed to resolve wasn't with a Prestige teammate," he said. "It was a Lochlin teammate. You can't believe him—"

"Stop. If there is anything you need to come clean about, this is your chance. Your *only* chance. What happened after I left Lochlin?" she asked. No, not asked. She demanded.

He rolled his head back and sighed. All the things he had hoped to brush under the rug were out there. He had known better. He hadn't lied, exactly, but he hadn't been truthful, and he knew from years of experience of dealing with witnesses that the truth always came out. Secrets never stayed buried.

"I was worried about you," he said. "So I tried to find you."

"Sounds like you were trying to stalk me."

He scoffed. "Would you please lower the gun before you accidentally shoot me?"

"If I shoot you," she said, "it won't be an accident. I am giving you one opportunity to tell me your side of this. That one chance is *now*. Talk."

Troy took a breath. "I was in love with you, and you disappeared without a word. I knew that was my fault. You left because of the incident with Sarah. Not only had I caused that by kissing you in the office, but... I had inadvertently led Sarah on."

Meri narrowed her eyes. "Inadvertently?"

He ground his teeth as regret caused his stomach to ache. "We were having drinks one night—me, Sarah, and Randall. I walked Sarah to her car because we were parked close to each other. She asked me what was going on with you and me. I told her nothing because you wouldn't cross that line. I jokingly said that I needed to get laid so I could get over you. It was a joke, but she..." Guilt rolled through Troy. "She asked me to go back to her place to see if she could help. We'd been drinking, and I was mad that you wouldn't give in to what I knew we were both feeling, and I..."

"You fucked her."

Though she was a master at hiding her emotions, he could hear the pain and betrayal in her quiet voice. He could see raw betrayal in her eyes.

He couldn't lie, so he nodded. "I did. And then I told her it couldn't happen again because it was against policy."

"But it did?"

"*No*. Goddamn it." He blew out his breath to tamper his frustration. "It happened that one time. I had too much to drink, and I was hurting, and… I made a mistake. She tried to convince me to see her again, but I refused. She went running to Randall, and he gave me five shades of hell and threatened to tell you. I promised him it was one time and would never happen again. I convinced him not to tell you. And I told Sarah that too. I made that clear to her."

"Oh, Troy," Meri said, her tone hard and bitter. "I don't think you did, because it all makes so much more sense now. Not just Sarah's anger when she caught us kissing but her words. The last thing she said to me was that she wasn't going to allow me to take you away from her. I thought she said that because when she told me she was interested in you, I said that you two couldn't date. She didn't say that because she thought I fabricated a company rule to keep you apart. She said that because she thought she already had you. She thought you were a couple."

"I told her it was—"

"Just sex," Meri said sarcastically. "With a teammate. While you also tried to sleep with your boss."

His gut twisted. "It wasn't like that. I was in love with you. Head-over-heels crazy in love, but Jesus Christ, Meri, you wouldn't budge. I didn't blame you. Our jobs were more important, I know that, but I couldn't stop wanting you, and knowing you'd never allow us to happen wore me down."

"It's my fault? Is that what you're saying? You *had* to

have sex with Sarah because I was desperately clinging to my integrity?"

"That's *not* what I'm saying," he said softly. "I'm not blaming you. Trust me, I know it's my fault. Sarah's death. Your quitting. Your leaving. It's my fault. That's why I was so determined to find you. I wanted to tell you the truth."

"We've been holed up together for days, Troy."

"I never had the chance—"

She widened her eyes. "If you had the chance to have sex with me upstairs, you had the chance to tell me the truth."

"Okay," he said. "I never had the *courage*."

She laughed flatly. "We talked about this. About what happened with Sarah. You told me she was going to file a complaint against me."

"That's true. That happened."

"Why didn't you tell me the full story right then?"

Damn it. Why hadn't he? Because he was a coward. That was why. "I didn't think you'd... You wouldn't understand why I turned to her when I wanted you."

She shook her head. "We were in an impossible situation, Troy. I might have been angry, but I would have understood."

"Meri," he pleaded.

"This isn't only about Sarah. What happened at the safe house, Troy?"

He narrowed his eyes, confused by her question. "I told you."

"You got a call, and when you showed up at the safe house, the Bantams had been slaughtered."

"Yes. That's true."

"Where were you when that happened?"

He didn't like the distrust in her voice. He also didn't like that she was still aiming her gun at him.

"I was a few blocks away. I never went far in case something happened. I wanted to be close to get to Logan."

She creased her brow as if whatever was on the tip of her tongue was too painful to say.

"Did you kill them?"

Troy felt his eyes bulge. "*What?*"

In all the years he'd known her, he'd never seen her show much emotion, but tears filled her eyes as she stared at him.

"Did you kill them and take Logan to get to me?"

Once again, he had the sensation that he'd been punched in the gut. "Are you serious?"

"I talked to Randall. I talked to Hank. And then I talked to Director Bruce. The only story that doesn't line up with the rest"—a tear fell down her cheek—"is yours."

His heart dropped to his feet. "Meri," he whispered. "No."

"You were stalking me," she said.

"No." He closed his eyes. "I was trying to find you, yes. Because—"

"You love me," she said flatly.

"I do."

She bit her lips and shook her head. "I want to believe you, Troy."

"Then believe me."

"I did the one thing I warned you all against. I thought with my heart, and I lost sight of the truth."

He definitely did not like where this conversation was going. "Listen—"

"If it had been Randall or Hank who had tracked me down and asked for my help, I would have helped them too," she said. "But I would have spent a lot more time verifying the truth. I took you at your word because I was so happy that you had come to me. I put my new team in danger. I asked them to break the law to protect you."

Panic filled his chest. "Just listen—"

"Three people—three reputable security professionals—think you're a danger to me and to Logan. They all asked me to take him back to Lochlin Private Security for his safety."

His gut tightened as the panic turned to all-consuming fear. "Oh, no. You didn't... Did you tell them where he is?"

"No," she said flatly. "I don't trust them either."

Either. The word cut him like a knife. "I became fixated on finding you," he said. "I know that. I took it too far until the director called me out. I was obsessed with finding you and fixing things so you could come back to work. I knew how much Lochlin meant to you, and I was the one who ruined it. That was on me. I was determined to make things right for you. Randall made it out to be much worse than it was. But once I was told to stop, I did."

"You didn't," she countered. "If you had, you wouldn't be here right now."

Oh, God. She wasn't listening. She wasn't hearing him.

"I stopped looking, but I didn't get rid of the information I'd gathered. When I started to suspect something was wrong with our team, I printed off what I had and deleted all my files so they couldn't track you. But I used that intel to start looking for you again. Just in case I needed to get Logan somewhere safe. I didn't lie about what happened to him or his family. And I didn't *murder* anyone, Meri. My God. How could you even ask me that?"

"Because I messed up," she said. Lowering her gun, she shrugged. Though she was no longer aiming the weapon at him, she didn't holster it. She was still ready to fire at him if needed. "I messed up when I didn't put an end to our dinners after I realized we were developing feelings. I messed up when I didn't stop you from kissing me. And I messed up when I didn't verify your story after you showed up here without warning. I keep misstepping where you are concerned, and I don't know the truth anymore."

"The truth is I love you and I messed up too. A lot. But I would give my life to protect you and that kid. I don't know what seeds were planted in your head, but if you can't trust me, then we're bound to make even more mistakes, and I can't risk that. It's time for Logan and me to hit the road."

"He's gone."

Once again, her words jolted him. "What?"

"I brought you inside so Lynn and Marta could take him somewhere safe. Don't worry. Prestige will protect him."

"You can't do that! You have no right!"

"I have every right. Until I know the truth about who is and isn't out to hurt that kid, I will do whatever it takes to keep him safe. Even if that means hurting you."

He couldn't argue with her logic. He would make the same call. But damn it, he never thought he'd be on the losing end of that.

"Are you going to turn him in?"

"Not until I know who to trust."

"You can trust *me*!"

Another tear rolled down her cheek. "I hope so. But until I can verify that, I have to consider that you could be a threat."

"A threat?"

"We agreed to put Logan first, remember? I'm getting too much conflicting information, Troy. I can't risk his life because of my personal feelings." She reached for the doorknob but then stopped and looked at him with those same sad eyes. "Don't try to find him, because if you succeed, I'll consider you a threat and shoot you."

"Hey," he called before she could leave. "What's your gut telling you?"

"That having my team step in to protect him is the right call. I don't believe you killed his parents, Troy. I don't believe you used him to get to me. But I can't risk being wrong. The price is too high this time."

"Meri," he called, but she yanked the door open and walked away. He followed her, determined to make her listen to him, but as he entered the living room behind her, Casey raised her gun.

"Stop right there," she warned.

Meri finally holstered her gun as she took Logan's backpack from Casey's other hand. Apparently Casey had collected his things while Meri held Troy at gunpoint.

"I didn't tell the director where to find you, but they are looking for you," Meri said. "If you're being honest, this is the time to turn yourself in and help Lochlin flesh out your mole. If you're not"—she shook her head sadly—"you should run, because they are closing in on you."

Troy stood motionless watching her leave. Something

about the way she turned her back on him felt so final. Like she'd given up on him. That broke his heart like nothing he'd ever felt before. How could she turn her back on him? How could she even consider what she was doing?

Casey's look was more sympathetic than sad as she kept her gun aimed at him. "This wasn't easy for her. She really does want to believe in you. But she's smart enough to know she could be thinking with her heart. Do the right thing for all of you, Troy. Let us protect Logan while you help Lochlin sort this mess out. Then you can come back to her." She backed out of the house and rushed down the stairs.

A moment later, a car pulled away.

Troy reached the window in time to see them disappear down the long tree-lined driveway.

"What the fuck just happened?" he yelled at the empty house.

[9]

Meri sat quietly as Casey drove her to the newest and, hopefully, last safe house she would be occupying with Logan.

"Thank you," she said. "For having my back."

"I always have your back, Meri," Casey said. "We all do."

"I don't mean with your gun."

"I know what you mean." Casey glanced at her. "You love him."

Meri looked out the window as they drove down yet another aimless street to see if they were being tailed. "I'm not sure that matters now."

"Of course it does. I can see how much your heart is hurting. Confronting him wasn't easy, but it was necessary."

She didn't dispute Casey's observation. Any other time, she'd scoff, laugh off the sentimental comment. She couldn't right now. Her heart *was* hurting. More than hurting, it was screaming at her for ruining everything she had been wanting for so long.

"He didn't do those things. I know he didn't. But..."

"But you're smart enough to understand that we never really know other people as well as we think we do. Everyone is capable of having a dark side that we don't or refuse to see."

Meri did know that. And she hated that she had to apply that knowledge to Troy. "What if he did do it, Casey?" she asked because she had to put her fear into words. "What if he hurt Logan's family to get to me? That little boy is never going to fully recover from what he's been through."

"No, he won't, but that isn't your doing. You are doing everything you can to help him. Even if Troy did hurt people, that isn't on you. You can't control what other people do, Meri. You know that. We all know that. If you are right, you probably saved Logan and maybe even yourself. If you're wrong, Troy will understand."

"Will he?"

"The decision you made was to protect a child."

"Yes. It was."

"Troy will understand, and he'll forgive you."

"I hope so."

Troy's face flashed through her mind. First, the sweet and seductive smiles he always gave her, even before they were lovers. Then, the hurt in his eyes as she stood with her weapon drawn, demanding answers from him. She'd cut him so deeply. But she had done it for Logan.

"Honestly, Meri," Casey said, "if he doesn't respect that you put Logan's needs above his, he isn't worth the time you're putting into feeling bad. This is what we do. This is what Troy does. He knows the score. If he doesn't, he's a piss-poor guard. And a selfish man."

Meri shook her head. "He isn't either of those."

"Then he'll understand because he would have done the same thing. Hell, I would do the same thing. If I thought for a moment you were putting Logan in danger, I'd snatch him from you too. His safety is the priority. Bottom line."

"Bottom line," Meri whispered. Though she knew Casey's pep talk was an attempt to take the edge off her guilt, it wasn't working. She knew, in her head, that she'd done the right thing. But her heart wasn't listening.

"So, Marta says that Logan is big into science."

Meri had to blink to follow Casey's sudden turn in the conversation. "Uh, yeah. He likes rocks and space. Things like that."

"I happen to know this super sweet nerdy guy who would love to hang out with a super nerdy kid sometime. How about Shawn and I bring pizza over one night? Shawn has a crazy rock collection. They can talk geology, and we can do exciting stuff, like monitor security cams." Casey's boyfriend wasn't just a nerdy scientist, he was on the team of medical examiners for the county. He was smart, clever, and knew that official business wasn't to be gossiped about. They could trust him to keep Logan's whereabouts a secret.

Meri smiled at the idea of how excited Shawn would be to have a captive audience, and how much Logan would eat up every word.

"That sounds great. Logan would love it."

"So would Shawn."

"Just remind Shawn that Logan is six. He should probably focus on how cool the rocks are instead of the petrographic analysis and mineral makeup."

Casey jerked her face to her passenger. "What the... *What*? You speak Shawn-inese?"

Meri wasn't expecting to genuinely laugh so soon after breaking Troy's heart again, but she did and was thankful to Casey for that.

"Sometimes."

"Nerd," Casey muttered.

On the outside of town, Casey pulled into the driveway of a house even smaller than the one where they'd left Troy angry and confused. This one didn't have the pond in front or the beautiful trees, but the yard was fenced in, and the houses were spaced out enough that the neighbors weren't on top of them. There was a deck, but it wasn't nearly as magnificent. This house wasn't the perfect fit the other had been, but it would do.

They walked in, and Meri immediately scanned the open concept, calculating her duck-and-cover plans for Logan. She had to think outside her normal box in case Troy was as bad as she'd been told. If he came looking for her and Logan, she didn't want him to find the boy by scanning the rooms.

She and Troy had always been able to finish each other's thoughts. The last thing she wanted was for him to be able to predict where she'd tell Logan to hide if shit went down.

Casey also went to work on learning the layout of the house, but Meri's focus changed when Logan screamed her name and jumped to his feet the moment he noticed her.

He came running across the living room as if he hadn't

seen her for days instead of an hour or so. Throwing his arms around her waist, he hugged her tight.

She smiled as she ruffled his hair with one hand and hugged him to her with the other.

He peered around her side before looking up at her. "Where's Troy?"

Yeah. She knew that was coming. Squatting down so she could look him eye to eye, she did her best to explain in terms he could understand. The confusion and little hint of fear in his eyes shattered what was left of her heart. She hated how much this poor kid had been through, and she hated that she was putting him through even more. Clearly he was expecting to hear some terrible news and was bracing himself for the worst.

She forced a reassuring smile to her face, hoping to put his little mind at ease.

"Troy is going to try to find the bad guy so we can stop running," she said. "We have to hunker down a bit longer, okay?"

"What if the bad guy gets him?" he whispered. The concern in his voice was genuine. The bond that had formed between Logan and Troy was as strong as any Meri had seen. Logan counted on Troy as much as a little boy could count on any adult.

"You know what? I don't think that's going to happen, because Troy is smarter and stronger than any bad guy I've ever met."

"Can I call him?"

"No, buddy. We can't call him. We still have to do our

best to be safe, and that means we have to be very careful where we go and who we call."

A pout turned Logan's mouth into a frown, but he didn't argue. He was probably one of the most compliant kids Meri had ever seen. For some reason, that made her sad. All the running and hiding and keeping secrets seemed to have dimmed the spark a kid his age should have.

She wished more than anything she could give his innocence back to him, but he'd seen too much darkness in his short life to ever convince him that life was always fun and games.

Taking his hands, she forced a big smile. "Once this is all over, I think we should get all the Prestige team and drag them to the park to play and have a big picnic. Don't you?"

He smiled. "And Troy?"

Meri swallowed. "And Troy, if he can come."

"Hey," Lynn interrupted. "Let's show Meri our escape plan."

Logan pulled Meri toward the second bedroom. There was a toybox below the window with clearly marked instructions with photos on how to open it in case of fire.

"If Troy was here, he'd tell me this is the way to escape."

Meri ruffled his hair. "Well, since Troy isn't here, I'm going to tell you that. If things get scary, you go out this window and run to a neighbor and ask them to call the police."

Questions filled Logan's eyes, and that hint of excitement that he'd managed to muster up faded away. "Nothing bad will happen, though. Not with you and Troy here."

Damn, she felt like a jerk. She was all but telling him not

to trust Troy, and that was the only person he'd trusted for weeks.

"I know it's confusing," she said. "You have so many rules to learn, and they are always changing, but this one is important. If you have to run away, I want you to talk to the neighbor and get help."

He stared at her, and the sense of distrust was palpable.

She didn't blame him.

"I want Troy," he said.

For lack of anything else to say, she smiled. "We'll see him soon."

"Okay," Logan said. "Can I play alone now?"

Damn it. He'd seen through her lies.

"Sure." She barely got the word out before he darted off. Facing Lynn, she sighed. "I know. I lied to a kid."

"You told him what he needed to hear to put his mind at ease. That's okay sometimes. How are you doing?"

"Honestly? I'm unsettled by how this day has gone."

"You made the right choice."

"I know." Meri was confident in that. "Until we can sort out the truth, we have to protect Logan. I know that."

"But?" Lynn asked.

Meri shrugged and let out a long, depressed sigh. "But I waited an awfully long time to have a life with Troy, and I probably blew it in less than a week."

"Do you think he did it?" Lynn asked. "Really?"

She shook her head. "No. I think there is a lot more to whatever happened after I left New York, but I don't know who to trust to get to the bottom of it. Even if I did, I don't think I can be objective. I want Troy to be innocent. My investigation is biased before I even begin."

"May I reach out to him? I'd like to hear his take on all of this. I can be more objective. Maybe I'll find something that you both overlooked."

"Yeah. Be careful. If he's as manipulative as my old teammates are making him out to be, he could twist you around too."

Lynn chuckled. "Do you know me at all? There's never been a man who can twist me around."

"Tell that to Justin," Meri said with a roll of her eyes and a sarcastic tone.

The look Lynn gave in return conveyed her displeasure at the accusation. "I'm going to have Joanie bring you food. Take a look around and text her if you need anything."

"Will do. Lynn," she called. "Thank you. I know this situation is taxing our resources and finances."

"He's a kid, Meri. We don't turn our backs on kids. We'll see this through and worry about the rest later."

Lynn left, and Meri bolted the door behind her. She could hear Casey and Logan chattering down the hall and was so thankful that she had her team. She couldn't think of a time that she'd needed them as much as she did now.

She had been honest when she said she was biased where Troy was concerned. She couldn't possibly sort all this out without her teammates taking a neutral stance to determine if Troy was capable of the things he'd been accused of doing.

Randall, Hank, and Director Bruce claimed to have seen a different side of him than she had. She was smart and confident in her ability to read people, so she couldn't fathom that Troy was the monster they'd made him out to be. But she'd also fallen in love with him a long time ago, and love has a way of blinding people.

As Casey continued talking with Logan, Meri walked the house, stopping at each window to take in the expansive yard on each side, noting any places that might provide cover for someone closing in on the house. Then she turned the blinds enough to peer through but not enough to make it easy for someone to see inside. A few days ago, the change of position in her blinds had tipped her off to someone hiding inside her house.

Little did she know then how her world would be turned upside down. Just a few hours ago, her upside-down world had been welcomed because it had brought Troy back to her. Now she was confused, uneasy about what she thought she knew, and she hated that feeling.

She wanted answers. She *needed* answers, but the only way to get them was to insert herself back into Lochlin Private Security, and she couldn't do that without putting Logan in danger. Though she wasn't good at relinquishing control, she was going to have to. This one time, she was going to have to let someone else solve a problem on her behalf.

Her problem—the one she had to focus on—was the danger facing that little boy down the hallway. Her broken heart and self-doubt were issues she'd have to deal with once Logan was safe.

Troy was sitting on the deck of the little pond house when two cars came down the driveway. He sat, looking at the water, sipping his coffee until the black sedans parked, and Director Bruce and several other Lochlin Private Security guards climbed out.

The other men stood by the car, keeping watch, while the director approached Troy. His footfalls echoed across the wood with loud steps that shook Troy down to his core.

He was used to Meri's steady but light steps and Logan's rushed clomping steps, but the steady fall of the director's expensive shoes and big feet unsettled him. Though the last few weeks had been tense and unpredictable, the last few days had eased his mind. Being with Meri again, even with Logan in tow, had brought him a sense of inner peace he wasn't expecting to find while on the run.

That peace had shattered a few hours ago. His world had shifted in a way that felt incredibly wrong to every instinct in him. He and Meri should have stuck together, but he couldn't blame her for leaving. Not if their entire Lochlin team had turned against him. And it seemed they had.

Troy had debated what to do once Meri and Casey had left. But Casey had all but told him what his choices were—prove to Meri that he hadn't done the things she'd been told by turning himself in. Any other action would prove, in her mind, that he was guilty. Somehow, Meri's perception of him was more important than whatever consequences he was about to face for his decision to slip from the safe house with Logan.

He had no idea what was coming now that the director

had arrived, but after the day he'd had, Troy was expecting the worst.

"Are you armed?" Director Bruce asked.

Troy nodded toward the guns beside him. "That's all I have."

The director removed the clips from Troy's guns and put his knife in his pocket. "I'm glad you called. This has gone on long enough."

Troy smirked. "I ran out of options. Coffee?"

"No, thanks." He looked around at the woods and the calm water. His black suit was out of place in this setting, but he wasn't as out of touch as his finely pressed clothing made it seem. He wasn't scanning the scenery. He was looking for danger. Though he was more of an office politician than an active guard these days, Ron Bruce was smart. That gave Troy hope. Hope that he was smart enough to see through whatever stories had gotten Meri so out of sorts.

"Nice place," the director said.

"I like it," Troy said before taking a sip of coffee. "It's quiet."

"Where is Logan Bantam?" Apparently, their small talk was done, and the director was moving on to the reason he was there.

Troy drew a long breath as he sat his mug on the small table he had put between two chairs so he and Meri could sit there and watch Logan play. However, since she had left, he had been sitting there, watching the pond and thinking about his actions.

Had he used Logan to convince her to let him back into her life? He couldn't deny how at home he'd felt being with the two of them. Nor could he deny that he had known that she might slam the door in his face, but she never would have left a little boy out to hang.

But he kept coming to the same conclusion. Despite his determination to find her, despite dragging her into Logan's situation, he wasn't the bad guy she had treated him like earlier. And he didn't think she believed he was. She was being careful. She was playing defense. She was doing exactly what he had done when he'd whisked Logan off in the first place.

"Meri took him," Troy answered. "Her new team is protecting him now."

"From whom, Troy?"

Sinking deeper into his chair, he scoffed. "She said she's not sure. Randall told Meri that I killed the Bantams and kidnapped Logan so that I would have a reason for her to help me."

"Did you?"

"No. Meri knows that I didn't, but she's got too much information to sort out, and until she does, she is making sure Logan is safe. Which, despite that being a bitter damn pill to swallow, is the right thing to do."

"She was always very smart, wasn't she?"

Troy wanted to laugh. Ron Bruce was clever, but his question was obviously a transparent attempt to lure Troy into some kind of trap to prove he'd been stalking Meri.

"Randall is wrong, Director. He was wrong about my reasons for trying to find Meri a year ago, and he's wrong about why I sought her out after I took Logan."

"So you aren't in love with her?"

"Oh, I'm in love with her. Head over heels, in fact. But I'm not insane, and I'm not a danger to her, Logan, or anyone else." He finally looked up at his boss and sighed at the disbelief in the director's eyes. "I was responsible for her decision to quit. I wanted to find her and try to right the wrong that made her leave. I'm not some obsessed psychopath."

"Well, the thing is, two of your teammates strongly disagree with that. Unfortunately, I'm beginning to suspect they are right."

He shrugged. "I went to you. I told you there was something off about the team, that something was going to happen."

"How did you know that?"

"My gut."

"Come on, Troy," the director said firmly. "You might as well tell me your tarot cards told you. I can't move a family based on gut feelings and instinct. I need facts. I told you that."

Troy fought the urge to jump to his feet. He didn't doubt that one of the guards standing nearby would take the movement as a threat and would be more than happy to put a bullet in him. Instead, he took a long breath and reminded himself to remain calm.

"That's bullshit, and you know it. Gut feelings save our asses far more than facts do."

"I'm not here to debate that with you. What was so off with the team that you *knew* something was going to happen to the Bantams?"

"Randall started spending money he shouldn't have had. I thought maybe he'd been bought off."

"He married into money."

Troy creased his brow. Randall got married? "No, he didn't—"

"Yes, he did," Director Bruce countered firmly. "He got married a few months ago, and we agreed he should keep his marriage secret for the safety of his wife."

"Why?"

"Honestly," the director said, "he was concerned about your fascination with Meri and your stability. He didn't want to share anything too personal with you."

Troy did his best not to roll his eyes. "I'm not—"

"We searched your apartment after you went on the run, Troy. We saw the pictures."

He wasn't following. "What pictures?"

"The hundreds of pictures that you had all over the damn walls. Meri at the store. Meri at her mother's. Meri jogging. Meri—"

He did stand then, ignoring the way the men by the car stood taller, more alert.

"I didn't have a single picture of Meri in my apartment. I had a handful on my phone, but that's it. I've never had a single *printed* photo of her."

The way Director Bruce stared at him, his face stoic, let Troy know he didn't believe him.

"There were pictures of that woman covering your walls," the director said. "You had been following her for months before she left, and when she disappeared you snapped. As evidenced by your obsession to find her."

Troy dragged his hand down his face. "You know what? My downstairs neighbor would know that this isn't right. Her name was Lucia Vega. She had a key to my place so she could water my plants. Find her. Ask her what my apartment looked like. She was in there at least three times a week to take care of the ferns my sister keeps bringing over. I can't keep the damn things alive."

Director Bruce continued staring at him.

"How are you not seeing that I'm being set up?" Troy insisted.

"Why would someone do that?"

"I don't know. Ask Randall."

"Troy," he said between clenched teeth, finally showing his frustration.

"Okay, maybe he did marry into money, but that doesn't mean he didn't get paid off by someone to kill the man who could take them down. Now he's pinning it on me."

"He didn't get paid off. *Nobody* got paid off. Do you honestly think two people got killed on our watch and we didn't turn over every rock on every person who knew where they were? We checked bank records, phone records, email, and text. Hell, we even looked into everybody's medical history. Nobody got paid off. Nobody has an offshore account. The only person who had a motive *and* the means to hurt those people was you. And that motive was your fixation on your former team leader."

"I told you I was trying to fix things—"

"Fix the fact that you slept with Sarah and were ultimately responsible for her death? Or stalking Meri? Or kidnapping a child under our protection? Which thing were you trying to fix?"

Exacerbated from repeating himself, Troy threw his hands up. "Call my neighbor—"

"It's not just the photos," Director Bruce stated. "You had file after file of Meri on your computer."

"No." He raked his hand over his hair. "I mean, yes, I did, but I deleted that file when I started to suspect there was a mole on our team."

The director puffed out his chest as he stood taller, clearly ready to play his ace. "You put hidden cameras in her apartment months before she quit. That had nothing to do with you trying to find her. You were *stalking* her."

That sensation of his stomach dropping to his feet was becoming way too familiar, but it hit him again. Confusion and fear clouded his mind, making it impossible to finish a sentence.

"Cameras... No... I didn't..."

"We found the footage on your computer. You had been watching her every move. For months. When did it start, Troy? How long had you been following her? How did you get cameras in her house?"

"I did not put cameras in her house," he demanded, his fear for Meri growing to match the concern he'd had for Logan.

"Let me guess." The director smirked. "I should ask Randall about that too."

Troy shook his head. "I... I don't know. I... Director, please... I didn't kill them. Someone is pinning this on me."

"Why would someone do that, Troy? You give me a motive, and I'll look into it."

He swallowed. He didn't know. He couldn't think of a

motive other than money. If it wasn't the Escobars paying for a hit, he didn't know why someone would try to frame him like this.

"Maybe someone was...you know...mad that I was assigned as team leader after Meri left. Hank and Randall have both been there longer than I have."

"Someone framed you for stalking, murder, and kidnapping a kid because they didn't want you to be their leader?"

That sounded lame, even to Troy. "Call my neighbor and ask about the photos. At least do that much. Please. If she tells you they weren't there before I disappeared with Logan, will you at least consider that I might be telling the truth?"

He hesitated before digging in his pocket. "What's her name again?"

"Lucia Vega."

Director Bruce pulled his phone from his pocket. "Sit down. Don't move."

Troy sank back into the seat he'd been occupying when the director had first arrived. He watched as his boss walked far enough away that his voice was muffled, but Troy still caught an occasional word.

Bruce asked someone to find a number for Lucia Vega, then tapped at his phone again. After several moments, he spoke. The wind carried his voice away, but Troy was watching his face. The director was uninterested at first, clearly not expecting to hear verification of Troy's story, but then he perked up as if surprised.

He talked for several more minutes before ending the call. He dropped the phone into his pocket and put his hands on his hips as he scanned the area. He seemed to be having some kind of internal debate. Finally, he returned to Troy.

"She verified your story and said her boyfriend could vouch for you as well. He went with her sometimes to check on your plants. She says the photos hadn't been in your apartment the day before we searched it."

Relief filled Troy. "So what are you going to do?"

"What I came here to do. Take you into custody."

Troy opened his mouth, ready to protest.

"I don't know what the hell is going on here," the director stated before Troy could make a fuss, "but until I figure it out, you're going to be in a holding cell."

"Don't take me back to New York," Troy pleaded. "Not when Meri and Logan are *here*. They could be in danger."

"You can't help them," the director said. "You need to focus on helping yourself."

"Incoming," one of the other guards called. With his gun in one hand, he raised the other, silently ordering the vehicle to stop, which it did. "Put your hands where we can see them!"

A moment later, the driver's side and passenger doors were opened by other guards.

The director watched two women climb from the car. "Who are they?"

"Lynn Sanchez and Casey Thombert. They work with Meri."

"Were you expecting them?"

"No. They're probably here to collect their equipment. They set up security around the property."

"Disarm them, then let them through," Director Bruce called to the other men standing guard.

Lynn stood with her usual emotionless stare as she said something. The man in front of her flashed his ID, and Troy had to chuckle. Of course she demanded verification before handing over her weapons. She and Meri must have been separated at birth, because Meri would have done the exact same thing.

Though he wasn't sure he could read Lynn's reaction as she headed his direction, Troy easily understood the satisfied smile on Casey's lips. He'd taken her advice and turned himself in. She was happy about that.

"Ladies," he said as they stepped onto the deck. He nodded toward the man beside him. "This is Director Ron Bruce of Lochlin Private Security. This is Meri's new boss, Lynn Sanchez, and her teammate Casey Thombert. I already unhooked your computers and cameras. They're on the table waiting for you."

"That was handy of you, Troy," Lynn stated.

"Needed to do something with my time. Since I'm not protecting my client."

She merely cocked her brow at him.

"Where's Logan Bantam?" the director asked her.

"In our custody until those responsible for killing his parents are found."

"You have no authority—"

"Have you verified that a member of your team didn't kill his family?"

When the director didn't respond, Lynn smiled. "He's

well protected and will continue to be protected until Meri says otherwise."

"Meri De Luca—"

"*Osborne*," Lynn and Troy corrected at the same time.

"I don't care what she changed her name to when she disappeared. She is no longer a member of this agency. If she does not hand Logan Bantam over in the next twelve hours, I'm going to report Logan missing to the authorities who will charge her with kidnapping and whatever else I can dream up. And you'll all be accomplices."

Lynn didn't so much as blink. Casey tilted her head and grinned. Her petite frame and big blue eyes gave the impression that she would be easily intimidated. She wasn't.

Director Bruce let out a frustrated sigh. "You have no idea what you are getting into."

"Actually," Lynn countered, "I'd be very interested in speaking with your supervisors. I'd like to know what their plan is to ensure that you are capable of overseeing your department and preventing anything like this from ever happening again."

Ouch.

"Well," Troy stated before Director Bruce could retort, "this is fun, but I have to get my things. I'm being *detained*."

"For your own good," the director said.

"May we go in and get our equipment?" Casey asked.

"Be my guest," the director stated. He opened the door and gestured for them to enter.

"What can I do?" Lynn quietly asked Troy as Casey headed inside.

"Someone is making it look like I stalked Meri," he

answered as softly. "They found photos in my apartment that weren't there when I left and footage of spy cams in her house on my computer. Someone had been watching her for months. Whoever it was is behind the rest. They are setting me up to take the fall. Lucia Vega, in apartment 205, has a spare key to my apartment. Meri knows the address."

"All that evidence will be cleared out before we get there, Troy. It probably already has been."

She was right. Damn it. "Can you spare Marta?"

"She isn't a licensed attorney."

"But she can assist mine and feed you and Meri information."

"Hey," the director snapped, "you want me to cuff you right now, big boy?"

Troy scoffed. "Asshole."

Lynn grabbed his arm when he started toward the house to stop him from stepping around her. "We're going to find out who did this. No matter who it is."

She may have meant that to be a warning if he was guilty, but he wasn't, so he took it as reassurance.

"I'm counting on that."

[10]

Meri felt sick to her stomach as she looked at the images Troy's attorney had shared with Prestige. Her old Lochlin teammates had told her that Troy had an obsession, but nobody had told her about walls covered in pictures of her. Then again, maybe they didn't know. If Director Bruce was as smart as Meri hoped, he had assigned a different team to do the search. A team that wasn't ready to pin all of this on Troy without questioning the evidence before them.

Beside her, Casey grabbed another slice from the half-eaten sausage-and-pepperoni pizza that she and Shawn had brought over.

"Lochlin tested the pictures for fingerprints, but whoever put those up likely wore gloves, which also seems to corroborate that it wasn't Troy," she said. "He wouldn't have worn gloves to put up pictures in his own apartment. He still thinks it was Randall, but there is no evidence that he or anyone else on the team was paid off. It doesn't look like money was the motive, but nothing else is making sense."

"This is insane," Meri whispered as she clicked the mouse to look at the next photo that Casey had downloaded. Even though Shawn had taken Logan to another room to look at rocks, they were keeping their voices down. Logan hadn't stopped asking for Troy, and Meri didn't want him to hear his name mentioned. "How could someone have taken all these pictures and I never noticed?"

"There's more," Casey said around the bite of pizza in her mouth. "There were spy cams in your apartment."

A surge of anxiety caused Meri's stomach to roll. "What?"

"The investigators found footage on Troy's computer," Casey said. "His attorney has requested access to the drive so we can dig into it, but so far that's been denied. Lochlin is playing hardball right now, so Marta is working on filing official requests. Which takes time, of course. Troy told Lynn someone had been watching you for months and put the footage on his computer to try to frame him."

Meri's breath caught in her chest, but then a memory flashed through her mind. When they were in the hotel, talking about why she'd left, he mentioned that he had been looking for her. She had a moment of panic, but he had reassured her that any evidence he'd found about her had been deleted.

"Troy said he wiped his hard drive when he suspected someone of being a mole. He thought he might have to run, and he didn't want anyone to know that he'd been looking for me. He printed off the information and wiped his drive. That footage would have gotten wiped too, right?"

"Yeah," said Casey. "It should have been."

"Randall said he'd been shadowing Troy's computer. That's how he knew how to find me. He used Troy's research. Could he have gotten into Troy's computer after he wiped it and planted that footage?"

Casey shrugged. "I guess it's possible. Shadowing is spying, really, but once he's in, there's no saying he couldn't have left something behind."

"Would there be evidence of that on Troy's computer? Some kind of digital trail?"

"I don't know, Meri. I mean, if he wiped his hard drive, he might have wiped all the evidence Randall hid in the background. If there is still evidence on that hard drive, whoever has Troy's computer is going to have to check. Do you trust anyone on the inside who could try to access those files?"

"I don't know." Meri sighed. "Troy doesn't trust any of them, and he was there to see all this fall apart. He would know better than I would. We need to have his attorney push harder on this."

Moving on to the next image of Troy's apartment, Meri frowned not only at how many pictures there were of her but how long she'd been followed without realizing it. The pictures of her images spanned over a long period. More than a few months. She knew because many of them weren't everyday snapshots, but work events including holiday parties, birthday luncheons, and one of their coworker's retirement dinners.

One image in particular caught her attention, though.

Meri zoomed in on an image of her talking to Randall. Two silver mylar balloons floated over a table in the distant background. Light reflected off the metallic *five* and *zero*. The image had to have been taken at Director Bruce's fiftieth birthday party that had been thrown at the office three weeks before Sarah's death.

"He wasn't there," she muttered. She tapped on the screen to draw Casey's attention to the image. "Troy was not at this party. This was the same day as his nephew's kindergarten graduation. He was in Maine with his sister and her kids." She smiled as if that had validated all that she knew. "He couldn't have taken this picture."

"Can you verify that?"

"This was taken inside a secured building. There would be a record of him signing in if he showed up. They can verify that. I have to call the director."

"That's too risky," Casey protested. "I'll call Marta."

"But the director can have those records pulled right now, Casey. Troy's attorney will have to make an official request to have those pulled. It will take too long."

"Meri," she stated firmly. "We are already tempting fate by coming here. It would be too easy for someone to follow us. Giving Director Bruce a chance to trace your call is too risky. We might as well hand Logan over to them."

"Okay." Sinking into a chair, she sighed. "But it could take days for his attorney to get the paper filed and approved. This is so damn frustrating."

"I know. Let's keep looking over these pictures. Maybe something else will stand out to you."

Meri blew out her frustration and started skimming the

images again. She didn't stop until she noticed one of her at her mother's house. The photo was taken from outside and through the big window that filled most of her mom's living room. This had to have been a holiday because Meri was standing next to her cousin. She usually only saw extended family on special occasions.

What really caught her attention, though, was the image in the corner of the window. A blue shirt or jacket was reflected in the glass. Troy had a blue Yankees sweatshirt that Meri loved to give him crap about. She was a Mets fan. That was one of the few things they couldn't agree on. Seeing the reflection made her heart flip over in her chest.

However, as she zoomed in, she realized that reflection couldn't possibly be Troy. The body was too small, too short, and too fair. Troy was a big guy and had the dark hair and naturally tanned skin of his Italian-born father.

"What the *fox*," Meri whispered.

"Huh?" Casey asked.

Meri wasn't sure if she was asking what Meri was cursing or why she'd randomly called out to an animal. She didn't bother clarifying. She was too busy zooming in on the image.

"Do you see that?"

"What?"

"That reflection."

They both leaned in. Though the image was pixilated, it was clear the person taking the photo wasn't Troy. The person wasn't even male. Whoever had taken that picture was a woman. And not just any woman. Meri recognized her jacket, her hair...everything about her even if it was blurred.

Meri exhaled loudly. "Holy..."

Casey frowned at her. "Is there a reason you're censoring yourself?"

"Troy's rules. No cursing around Logan."

"He's in the other room."

"I know," she muttered and waved her hand dismissively. "Can we focus on this? That's Sarah Brewer. My teammate who died."

"The woman that Troy dipped his stick in when you weren't available?"

Meri glared at her. "Do you want me to hurt you? Because I *will* hurt you."

Casey lifted her hands as if to surrender. "Just clarifying."

Sighing, Meri nodded. "Yes. That's the one."

"Why would she be taking pictures of you?"

Meri rolled this new bit of information around for a moment before shrugging. "Because she was obsessed with Troy, and she couldn't have him."

"Because he loved you."

Meri rubbed her fingertips into her eyes. "That's the only thing that makes sense, right?"

"Yes, I agree," Casey said. "Look at these pictures. In most of these, you are with men. Men who are not Troy. Dollars to doughnuts she was hoping to catch you being intimate with one of them so she could prove that he was wasting his time fawning over you."

"Where were the cameras in my apartment placed?"

"Living room and bedroom. Was she ever in your apartment without you?"

Tucking her hair behind her ear, Meri thought back

before nodding. "I had cookouts at least once a month when the weather permitted. For teambuilding. She could have gone inside to use the restroom at any one of those gatherings. But she's dead, Casey. She didn't put those pictures in Troy's apartment, and she didn't dump the footage on his computer. Someone else had to have accessed that."

Casey shrugged. "If Randall could shadow Troy's computer, he could probably shadow Sarah's as well. He could have pulled these files to frame anybody he wanted. He chose Troy."

"Troy made it easy because he was determined to find me. He said it wasn't as bad as Randall made it out to be. Maybe he blew things out of proportion to set Troy up. I mean, it was Randall who turned Troy in for looking for me in the first place."

Pushing herself up, Meri paced for several long seconds before shaking her head. "He had to have started planting seeds of doubt in everyone's minds months and months ago. But why? The director told Troy there was no money trail leading to Randall or anyone else on the team. What did Randall have to gain by killing the Bantams and framing Troy?"

"Didn't he also tell Troy that Randall recently got married? Maybe the money trail leads to his wife."

"He married into money," Meri said softly, repeating what the director had relayed to Troy. "Son of a..."

"Can't say that either, huh?"

"I'm calling the director," Meri stated, ignoring Casey's question.

Casey frowned. "You better talk fast. If he's tracing his

calls, it won't take them long to figure out which cell towers you're using and narrow down your location."

Meri pulled her burner phone from her pocket and scrolled for the number she had saved to call the director. As soon as he answered, she started speed-talking.

"This is Meri. Listen carefully. There's a photo of me at your birthday party last year on Troy's wall. Check Troy's entry records into the office. He wasn't there. He took a vacation day to be with his family. He flew out to Augusta, Maine, the night before your party and came back Sunday afternoon. There's a little airport there, you can check the records."

"How do you—"

"There is another photo taken outside my mother's house. In the bottom right-hand side of the window is a reflection in blue. Blow it up, and you will see that it was Sarah taking that picture."

"Sarah?"

"Sarah also had access to my home on numerous occasions to plant cameras. Randall admitted to me that he had shadowed Troy's computer. He could have shadowed Sarah's as well. If he was able to hack his way in, it's possible he also took the footage from Sarah's computer and put it on Troy's."

"Meri, how do you—"

"You told Troy that Randall married into money. Check to make sure that money didn't arrive in his wife's bank account. That would give him motive to pin all this on Troy."

"It is after nine p.m. my time, Meri," he finally managed to state. "This could have waited until morning."

"No, sir. It can't. You've been holding Troy for days. He

didn't do this. He didn't do any of this. He's right. I bet if you think back, you'll realize it was Randall subtly making you doubt Troy all along. Everything goes back to Randall. Now you get your ass to the office and start looking into what I told you. *Please*," she added sarcastically before she ended the call and lifted a brow at Casey. "Fast enough?"

"Fast enough. But do you think that's going to get them to release Troy? He did take Logan without notifying the agency."

"Marta says Troy's attorney is really pushing that he was acting in the best interest of his client. I'd say that if they can poke holes in the theory that Troy was some kind of mad stalker and someone else did these things, they will have to let him go."

Casey didn't look nearly as convinced as Meri was, but she didn't let that deter her. Troy's innocence would be proven, and he'd be released by morning. She had to believe that, even if Casey didn't.

DAWN HAD BARELY BROKEN WHEN TROY WAS HAULED from his holding cell to the visiting area of the jail where he'd been housed for days. He was expecting to see his attorney, but Director Bruce sat at the table, looking like he hadn't gotten much more sleep than Troy had.

"Sit," the director ordered.

Troy dropped into a chair and sighed. He was getting really tired of these stupid games. Instead of pressing him to confess, the director put a photo of Meri and Randall in front of him. Troy looked it over for a moment before shrugging at the director.

"What am I looking for?"

"Do you recognize that image?"

Frustrated, he sighed and pushed the photo away. "You woke me up for this? How many more times do I have to tell you that I didn't take those pictures before you start listening?"

"I'm listening now."

Creasing his brow, Troy tilted his head a bit, trying to process what he'd heard.

"You weren't in the office the day that photo was taken," Director Bruce said. "We verified that your badge was never used to enter the building that day and that you had boarded a plane to Maine the night before. Granted, you could have driven back in that time and used someone else's badge, but your sister confirmed you attended her son's kindergarten graduation and offered photos to prove it." Sitting forward, Director Bruce slid another photo across the desk. "Look at this one. See the reflection off to the side here?"

Troy narrowed his eyes, trying to make out the image, but the director added a blown-up and slightly blurry copy.

"Is that Sarah?" Troy lifted his face, confused by this new information. "Sarah was following Meri?"

"We're still digging into this, but in this picture, this one image outside Meri's mother's house... It looks an awful lot like Sarah Brewer took this."

"But that doesn't explain how this got in my apartment."

"Exactly. We looked deeper into the spy-cam footage. We can't determine who dumped it on your computer, but the videos were dumped all at once and *after* you had gone on the run but *before* we searched your apartment. Seems awfully strange, don't you think?"

Troy was hesitant to feel relieved. He clung to his poker face, not sure what was going to happen next. After three days of answering endless questions, being accused of stalking Meri, and threatened with life in prison for murdering the Bantams and kidnapping their son, he wasn't going to let his guard down for a second. This could be a trap.

"I have two investigators checking every security and traffic camera around your apartment building. If one of our own broke in to put up those photos and dump that footage, we might be able to catch them."

"Meri called," he added.

Finally, Troy perked up. He didn't mean to. He should have been more guarded where Meri was concerned, considering they thought he'd murdered two people as an excuse to get close to her.

"How's Logan?" he asked, a quick attempt at excusing his sudden interest.

"I don't know. She didn't mention him. She's the one who tipped me off that you hadn't been at my birthday party. I had forgotten about that. She also pointed out the reflection in the glass and said that Randall admitted to hacking into your computer. We haven't been able to confirm that, but those computer nerds down in IT confirmed there was spyware on your hard drive. Now, it is possible," he said, "that Randall compromised your computer."

"That he dumped the footage," Troy clarified. "Goddamn it. I told you this days ago. Have you told Meri's team that you confirmed this? Randall is there. Who knows—"

"I spoke with Randall two days ago after you told me he had rented a house so close to Meri's. He was told to return to New York."

"Has he?"

The director sighed. "I'll have someone check. But I really don't think—"

"You said you verified he hacked into my computer."

"I said we verified there was spyware. We didn't verify it was Randall."

"He followed me—"

"He said he followed you to try to locate and return Logan Bantam." The director wasn't giving an inch.

Troy shook his head. "Director, he is lying."

"I'm bringing Randall in for further questioning as soon as I verify he's back in New York. Now if you are done huffing and puffing, there is something that I need from you. You say you've been acting in Logan's best interest. I need some kind of proof of that."

"Like what?"

"I need to hear Logan and verify he's okay. You're going to call Meri, and you're going to put it on speakerphone so I can hear him. And you better hope to God that he doesn't say anything that makes me think you had any motive other than protecting him. Understood?"

"Understood."

The director slid the phone that Prestige had programmed for Brian Donnelly across the desk. *How was that just over a week ago?*

"You want me to call now? It's four o'clock in the morning their time."

"You want to go back to your cell and wait for a more polite time?"

Troy flipped the phone open and selected the number for Brenda. Three rings in and Meri answered. Troy's heart lifted at the sound of her voice, even though it was groggy from sleep.

"Troy?" she asked.

He smiled. "I'm here."

"Did they let you go?"

"Not yet, but I think we're getting there."

She exhaled loudly into the phone. "How are you doing?"

"Oh, I've been better," he said lightly. "The bed is lumpy, the food is terrible, and my roommate snores."

"I'm so sorry. I had to—"

"I know." He lost his teasing tone. "Don't apologize. I get it. Listen, I need to talk to Logan."

"He's sleeping."

"Put him on," the director ordered. "I need to know that he's okay."

"Okay," Meri said. "Hey, Logan. Troy's on the phone. He wants to talk to you."

Closing his eyes, Troy could actually envision the scene playing out on the other end of the line. No doubt Logan was curled up against Meri, seeking the safety that had been so lacking in his life.

A moment later, Logan's tired voice came through the phone. "Troy?"

Troy couldn't stop the big grin that curved his lips. He also couldn't stop his heart from aching. He'd missed that kid as much as he'd missed Meri.

"Hey, buddy. How are you?"

"I was sleeping."

"I know. It's a really bad time to call, but this was the only time I had. I'm sorry."

Logan yawned. "Are you coming back soon?"

"I'm going to try. Are you doing okay?"

"Yeah. I got to look at some really cool rocks today. Well, yesterday, I guess."

"That's awesome."

"Casey's boyfriend is really smart, and he said he can teach me all kinds of things about science. He has more rocks than anybody I've *ever* seen." The sleepy sound faded with each word he said as his excitement grew. He was waking up. Meri would have a heck of a time getting him back to sleep now. "Meri said we might get to go to a park tomorrow. I've been practicing calling Meri *Mom*, but I keep forgetting."

"That's okay. It's hard to remember," Troy said, but he didn't think Logan heard.

The kid barely took a breath before he started rambling again. "When are you coming back?"

Troy chuckled when Logan finally stopped talking. "As soon as I can, bud."

There was muffled talk in the background, and Logan moaned in displeasure. "Meri says I have to go now."

"I'll talk to you again real soon. Try to go back to sleep, okay?"

"Okay."

"Hey," Meri said, coming back on the line. "He's fine. He and Shawn became fast friends. Casey suggested a trip to the park to let Shawn help him with rock hunting to start his own collection. I think it will be okay."

"Sounds like it," Troy said. "How are you?"

"I'm good," she said, but she didn't sound okay. She sounded upset.

Troy didn't have to think too much to know why. As much as he hated having her question him, she had to have hated it as well.

"Thanks for calling in last night," he said. "They were able to clear me of a few things at least."

The director cleared his throat. "I'm dropping the charges."

"You are?" Meri and Troy said at the same time.

"Logan is clearly eager for Troy to return. At this point, there is mounting evidence that Troy was set up, even if we don't know by whom. I have no reason to believe he's a danger to the kid. We'll get him out of here."

Troy nodded his thanks. "Am I free to go back to them?"

Director Bruce sat back and frowned. "Until we know who killed his parents and why, he could still be in danger. As the lead guard responsible for keeping him safe... I guess you better get your ass back there and keep him safe."

Troy smiled. "Thank you."

"But," he said, pointing a finger at Troy, "Meri De Luca is no longer employed by this company. She has no business working with you on this."

"Sir," Meri stated.

"However," the director continued, "these circumstances

are unusual. And...Meri was always a much better investigator than you are, so I'm going to let her involvement slide. This *one* time. You need to understand, Meri, that you are no longer employed by Lochlin, and you have no authority to act in that capacity. Your role in this is to assist Troy in keeping Logan safe. Do you understand?"

"Yes, sir," she answered.

"You'll check in with me every day," Director Bruce continued. "You will not go rogue again. If you need to move, you *will* tell me where you are."

Troy nodded. "What about Randall?"

"I'll keep you posted."

That was all he could ask for. "Hey," he said to Meri. "Tell Logan I'm coming home."

"He's going to be thrilled," Meri said. "He's missed you."

Troy hoped she had missed him too, but he couldn't really ask that when Director Bruce was listening in on their conversation. He would ask when he got back, though. He hoped that her working so diligently to prove to the director that Troy was innocent meant that she'd forgiven him for the one crime he had committed—lying about his relationship with Sarah.

"I'll get him on the first flight out," the director said. "You have means to pick him up from the airport?"

"I'll send someone."

"Good enough," Director Bruce said. "Let's get you released."

"I'll call back with details," Troy said.

Meri hesitated, but when she spoke, she sounded sincere. "I'll be waiting."

For the first time in days, Troy allowed himself to really breathe. He was going back to Logan and Meri. Back where he belonged. And the director was finally hearing him. Randall might have outsmarted his team for a long time, but that time was coming to an end, and Troy couldn't be happier about that.

[11]

The sound of gravel crunching under tires caused Meri's heart to flutter. He was back. Troy was back. She was as excited as she was nervous. They were going to have to deal with what had transpired the last time they'd seen each other. He might understand that she'd done what she had to do, and she might understand that he had turned to Sarah out of loneliness, but understanding didn't mean there wasn't underlying resentment on both of their parts waiting to show itself.

Those emotions had to be dealt with swiftly so they didn't interfere with protecting Logan. Or, hopefully, getting their very young relationship back on track.

"Hey," she called to Logan.

He turned from where he sat eating a big bowl of cereal in front of the television. She smiled when he used his sleeve to catch a dribble of milk running down his chin.

"Troy's here."

He jumped up, mouth full, and ran for the door. He

grabbed the knob before he stopped, as if remembering the rules, and looked at Meri. She peered out the window and verified it was Joanie and Troy climbing from the car.

"Go ahead," she said.

Logan unlocked the door and yanked it open. He was gone in a flash. A moment later, as she watched through the paned glass, he ran toward Troy. Troy smiled and opened his arms. In a scene that felt way too comforting to Meri, she watched him scoop the boy up and hug him tight.

She'd never wanted kids before, but after a week with Logan, she was beginning to think she might be an okay mom someday. The thought struck something in her that made her have to look away from the reunion happening outside.

Picking up his bowl, she used the remote to turn off the cartoon that he'd been glued to and busied herself with cleaning up what was left of his breakfast. She had no doubt that he'd be too distracted to eat now. Troy had only been gone a few days, but Logan had a long list of things he couldn't wait to tell him.

"Good morning," Joanie sang out, coming inside.

Meri flashed her a smile as she focused on rinsing out the sink. "Morning. Thanks for giving Troy a lift."

The door opened and Logan darted in. "Meri! He's back!"

"I know," she said. When she finally found the courage to lift her gaze to Troy, her heart started aching for him all over again.

He dropped a duffel bag by the door and shrugged out of the light jacket he was wearing. That hadn't been in his limited wardrobe before. He must have taken the time to swap out his clothes while in New York. Which meant he'd gone to his apartment and possibly seen some of the planted evidence for himself.

The exhaustion was evident in his slower movements, and when he looked at her, she could see it plainly written on his face. No doubt he hadn't been sleeping well. Wherever they had detained him was not conducive to getting a lot of rest. His shoulders stooped a bit lower than before he'd left, and the stubble on his face was proof he hadn't been given much opportunity to take care of himself.

God, she felt like an asshole for doing that to him.

Troy looked at Joanie, and she turned her focus on Logan as if they had this moment planned.

"Hey," she said in a super happy voice, "did you get a chance to look at all the new books I brought over?"

Logan's wide grin grew. "They are awesome!"

"Come on," Joanie said, holding out her hand. "Show me."

"Troy, come see."

Troy offered him a smile as he ruffled his hair. "Hey, buddy. I've been traveling for a long time. I'm going to take a nap, and then you can show me all your new stuff, okay?"

Logan looked a bit deflated, but Joanie worked her magic and told him she couldn't wait any longer. She *had* to see his new books. Logan ran toward his room, dragging her behind him.

Meri bit her lip when they disappeared before focusing on Troy again. "Well, that was a little transparent."

"I wanted to settle things between us."

Her chest tightened. He didn't sound angry—he even

said he wasn't—but she didn't know how he couldn't be. She'd held him at gunpoint. "I am so sorry—"

"I'm the one who is sorry, Meri. I should have told you about Sarah."

"I understand why you didn't," she said. "Things would have gotten more complicated."

"And I understand why you took Logan. He comes first. Always. We agreed."

She nodded. "This job is a bitch sometimes, huh?"

"Sometimes," he agreed. "Are you mad at me?"

"No," she quickly insisted. "Are you mad at me?"

He laughed softly. "No. I was a little peeved at first, but once I thought about your position, I knew you did the right thing."

"You look like hell."

Dragging his hand over his hair, he let out a long breath. "I feel like hell."

She gestured behind her. "You should shower and get some rest. The master bedroom is at the end of the hall. There are towels and—"

He took a big step and cupped the back of her head. Yanking her to him, he covered her mouth with his. Though his face was covered with sharp bristles, she melted into him and parted her lips. She'd been so worried that he'd hate her or blame her for what he'd been through that they'd never recover.

That concern had nagged her more as she and Logan had eagerly waited for his return. So she'd accept the prick of his beard on her skin as part of her comeuppance. If this was the price, she'd pay it.

Clinging to him, she deepened the kiss even more.

Finally, he leaned back and rested his forehead to hers as he caught his breath.

"Where's this shower you speak of?" he asked. "I definitely need it."

"Get your things."

He grabbed his bag, and she led him deeper into the house. The place was small, but the master bedroom had an attached bathroom with an amazing shower. She guided him inside the room, intending to leave him to do a little self-care, but he closed the door behind him and dropped his bag on the bed.

"It's Randall," he said as he unzipped his bag. "I have no doubt about that now. Do you?"

Meri watched him dig inside and pull out fresh clothes, a can of shaving cream, and a razor. "I think the money Ana—or whatever her name really is—was for the deed he did. She got the money, and then they got married so it wasn't tied to him. He killed them," Troy said and shook his head. "I mean, I knew that, but now I *know* that. And knowing it is blowing my mind." He looked at her and grinned lazily. "Pretend that made sense. I'm too tired to think before speaking."

"It made perfect sense."

With his clothes and toiletries in one hand, he slid his other arm around her waist, pulled her against him, and kissed her again.

"I can't decide what I should do first. Sleep, shower, or make love to you."

Contentment filled Meri as she dragged her hands over his arms and around his shoulders. "Sleep. Then shower.

Because I want you rested—and clean-shaven—before you make love to me."

"Yeah, but see, we have someone watching Logan right now, and she promised to stay as long as needed for us to work this out. Seems like a waste to not take advantage of that."

Meri couldn't argue with that. One thing she had learned over the last week was that when they got a chance to be alone, they really needed to enjoy that time. She untangled from him and walked into the bathroom. Though the room was small, there was enough room for her to slowly lift his T-shirt over his head and toss it aside. As she focused on releasing the button of his jeans, Troy kissed her head.

"I was so worried about you," he whispered. "If anything had happened to you—"

"I can take care of myself." She eased his zipper down before looking up to meet his eyes. "And anyone else who needs me."

"I know." Holding her face, he kissed her lightly. "But I was still worried. I can't lose you again."

"You won't," she whispered.

Dipping his face down, he tasted her lips. "Promise?"

"Come on, Troy," she said, pushing his pants over his hips. "You know we can't make promises like that in our line of work."

"Promise anyway."

Creasing her brow, she stopped removing his pants and focused on his face.

He wasn't telling her something.

"What's this about?" she asked. "What happened?"

Draping his arms over her shoulders, he exhaled heavily. "I found out...Sarah was watching you."

"I know."

"I don't know why," he said. "But all I've been able to think about was how close she could have been to hurting you because of me."

Meri shook her head. "Honey, I don't think she meant to hurt me. I think she was hoping to find something to make you change your mind about me."

Brushing his hand over her hair, he exhaled loudly. "That would never happen."

Meri smiled. "I know." Pushing his jeans over his thighs, she kneeled down to remove them and toss them aside. She smirked as goose bumps rose on Troy's skin as she lightly trailed her fingertips up his thighs, hips, and sides as she regained her footing.

Sinking her teeth into his bottom lip, she suckled it for a moment before releasing it and laughing.

"Are you sure you have the energy to shower?"

"No. But we're going to anyway. I missed you more than I missed sleep."

She smiled as she rested his head against hers. She'd always known they would be good together—perfect together—and they were. In every way.

"I love you," she whispered.

He smiled at her in the mirror. "I love you." Wrapping his arms around her waist, he kissed her shoulder much more gently than he had before. "If I don't shower now, I'm going to pass out."

Meri waited outside the bathroom as he showered. After

he dried and put on clean clothes, he collapsed on the bed. By the time she picked up the clothes he'd carelessly dropped, he was snoring. She could have stood there all day watching him sleep but decided she should relieve Joanie from babysitter duty and, she guessed, put Logan's mind at ease. He'd been so eager to see Troy, he would be disappointed that he was asleep already.

However, when she left a sleeping Troy and stopped at Logan's doorway, she found he had dozed as well. He'd been so excited to see Troy that he hadn't gone back to sleep after they'd been woken by a call in the middle of the night.

Joanie was putting his books back on the shelf as he lay curled in a little ball on his side. Easing into the room, Meri tucked the blanket up. She had learned that if he got the least bit chilled, he would wake, seeking comfort from her or Troy. It didn't take much to pull him from sleep.

She brushed his hair from his forehead and lightly laughed at the way he heaved a big breath. Despite everything that he was going through, he looked so at peace while he was sleeping. That gave her hope that he could fully recover one day.

When she turned, she spotted Joanie standing there with that annoying know-it-all smirk on her face.

"I knew it," Joanie whispered.

"What?"

"Under all those hard glares and sarcastic retorts, you really are a big mama bear."

The words made Meri's heart ache inexplicably. She looked at Logan one more time before leaving him to his nap.

Sitting at the little table, she raked her fingers through her hair and sank low in her chair.

"What's wrong?" Joanie pressed.

"I'm worried about him. I don't know what's going to happen to him. He has seen so much darkness in his short life. That can cause a lot of long-term damage."

"He'll need to talk to someone," Joanie agreed, sitting next to her.

Meri couldn't quite understand the gloom that was settling over her. As soon as the director found concrete evidence against Randall, he would be arrested, and this would all end. Now that he was actually looking into Randall, that wouldn't take long. Then Logan could stop running.

She should be thrilled, but she was even more terrified for him now. "He counts on Troy so much to feel safe."

"He counts on you, too. He thinks you're the bee's knees," she said lightly.

Meri laughed, but the ache in her heart grew. "I don't know if he has any other family to take him in, or if... What if he ends up in the system?"

Joanie put her hand on Meri's arm as if to comfort her. "He'll be okay. Lochlin won't let him slip through the cracks after all this. He's going to be taken care of."

"I certainly hope so. He's going to need a lot of care and attention to move forward." She glanced at Joanie when she didn't respond. The look on her face was almost as distraught as what Meri was feeling. "What's wrong?"

"Lynn said she was afraid you were going to go back to New York when this case ended. You are, aren't you?"

She opened her mouth but couldn't find the words.

"You and Troy worked everything out?"

"Yeah."

"And he's been cleared of all charges."

Meri nodded.

"So he'll leave. And Logan will leave. And you'll leave." Tears filled her eyes.

"Don't do that," Meri insisted. She heaved a sigh. "I don't know what's going to happen. To any of us."

Joanie pouted, but before she could make Meri feel worse, her phone rang. She stood and put it to her ear. "This is Joanie." She listened for a moment before turning and looking wide-eyed at Meri. "I'll let them know," she said after a minute. As soon as she hung up, her mouth gaped open like a fish several times before she found her words. "That was Lynn."

"What's wrong?"

"She got a call from Justin. Someone reported a disturbance at Randall's house."

"And?"

Joanie looked shocked. "They're dead. Randall and Ana are dead. It looks like Randall shot her and then took his own life."

Meri sank back in her chair. "Oh my God."

"He must have learned that Troy was released and realized the walls were closing in on him," Joanie said, retaking her seat at the table.

"It's over, then," Meri said. "It's really over."

Joanie nodded. Both seemed to share the same mixed emotions.

Meri looked down the hallway. "Poor Troy. He just fell asleep, but he'd want to know this right away."

"Go. Tell him."

Meri pushed herself to stand. "I told Lynn, and I'm telling you. No matter what happens next, we're family, and we'll always be family."

"Even if you leave?"

"Yeah. Even if I leave."

Joanie smiled, but Meri could see the shimmer of tears in her eyes.

"Go get Troy. Wrap up this case so you can...so you can go home."

Now that Troy wasn't concerned with getting arrested for kidnapping Logan, he was able to show up at Randall's rental home without being arrested. He was pissed as hell when Meri told him what had happened. Randall had gone to great lengths to frame Troy, and the prick wasn't going to pay a damn bit of the consequences for that.

Some might say death was enough punishment for his bad deeds, but to Troy, that felt like he'd taken the easy way out. Coward.

"What do you have?" Troy asked when Justin approached him to give him access to the scene. He didn't know if Justin was the officer in charge, but he had met Lynn's friend, so he wasn't too concerned if he was stepping on someone else's toes. He trusted Justin to talk to him.

"Welcome back," Justin said, shaking Troy's hand.

"Looks like a classic murder-suicide. Randall shot his wife, then himself."

"Was there a note or anything?"

"No, but follow me." He led Troy into a small bedroom and handed him a glove as he gestured to the desk.

Troy snapped the glove into place as he stood over the desk. He flipped several pages of notes in Randall's messy handwriting. The man had definitely been thorough in detailing all the reasons why he thought Troy was responsible for the Bantams' murders.

The one thing Randall had circled over numerous times was a question: *How did Troy get into the house unnoticed when Deon and Powell were on duty?*

Troy stared at the scribbled note—the one hole in Randall's theory—and realized that was a question he hadn't answered either. There were supposed to always have been two guards on site. That night, the two were the newbies—Deon and Powell. They were green, but they were smart and careful.

How had a murderer gotten by two guards to torture and kill clients? The killer hadn't snuck in, popped the Bantams, and disappeared. They had been tortured. That took time.

Where were Deon and Powell?

Troy hadn't stuck around the scene long enough to question them about what they'd seen or heard. He hadn't stuck around long enough to ask anyone anything other than where Logan was. But Randall was right. How did the murderer get in and do what he had done without being noticed?

Pulling his phone from his pocket—his real phone, not the flip phone Brian Donnelly had been using—he called the director. He continued skimming Randall's notes as he updated Director Bruce on where he was and why.

"What the hell is happening, Troy?" the director asked.

Troy stopped sorting through Randall's papers. "Who questioned Deon and Powell after the Bantam murders?"

"Hang on," the director muttered. He must have been checking his files because Troy could hear him clicking away on his keyboard. A few minutes later, he said, "Hank questioned the other teammates. By then, they realized you and Logan were gone and Randall was trying to locate you."

"Did they explain why they didn't see or hear anything?"

"They were checking the outside perimeter."

"At the same time?" Troy said. "That doesn't read right, sir. They knew better. One of them should have been indoors with the family at all times."

"They were new—"

"They still knew better," Troy insisted. "Call them all in. Deon, Powell, and Hank. I want to have a conference call with them now that I can question them myself."

"I'll call you when they're here," the director said.

Troy had barely hung up when a man came into the room. The nervous energy radiating from him was more than Troy, in his overly exhausted state, was prepared to handle. The guy must have had an entire pot of coffee all on his own.

"Justin," he said excitedly, "you're going to want to see this."

Justin turned to face him. "Hey, Shawn, this is Troy Buchanan."

Shawn creased his brow. "Meri's Troy?"

Troy grinned. He'd been called worse things. "You must be Casey's Shawn."

"Yeah, nice to meet you. I mean...maybe not given the circumstances, but... Hey, at least you're not in jail anymore, right?"

"What's up, Shawn?" Justin asked, putting an end to the man's fast rambling.

"I don't think this is as cut and dry as we initially thought. Come on." He disappeared from the office, leaving Troy with a confused look as he stared at Justin.

"He's brilliant despite being fairly socially awkward and slightly hyperactive," Justin said. "Casey thinks it's cute."

Troy chuckled as he followed Justin from the room to where Shawn had squatted next to Randall.

Shawn pushed his glasses up and smiled. "Here." He pointed with a gloved finger at Randall's wound. "Most self-inflicted gunshot wounds are made at contact." He put his finger to his own head, pressing against his temple as if he were holding a gun to his head. "Like so. Having the barrel against the skin would send the bullet straight through. But look at the angle on his wound." Shawn left his finger pointed but tilted his head to the side. "The bullet entered when he was leaning away. If he was having reservations about killing himself, he probably would have lowered his hand like so"—he mimicked the motion—"not pulled away from the gun."

"Maybe he was moving the gun and accidentally fired."

Shawn shook his head. "I considered that, but look at this," he said, clearly excited by his findings. He lifted Randall's right hand. "Those are defensive wounds, and they are fresh. He fought back. He punched whoever was trying to kill him, at least once, maybe twice."

Troy creased his brow. He agreed with Shawn's logic, but he was at a loss as to who would kill Randall.

"Search for security cams in the area," Justin called. "This might be a homicide."

Just like that, the already busy crime scene started buzzing with activity. While other officers looked for cameras, Shawn went back to reevaluate Ana's body. She'd been killed with one bullet to the head while she'd sat at the table. A half-eaten sandwich still sat on the plate in front of her body. She hadn't had a chance to react before being killed.

Shawn examined her wound and pointed. "Whoever shot her was standing about right there."

Troy stepped to where Shawn was pointing. He was directly in front of her body. She would have been looking right at whoever shot her. There was no way that she had been ambushed.

"Could she have been moved?" Troy asked.

Shawn nodded. "Possibly, but the angle of her entry wound implies she was sitting or someone extremely tall shot her."

Troy blew out a long breath. "If Randall didn't kill her, then it was someone she was comfortable with," he said. "She wouldn't be sitting at the table eating lunch if there was a known threat in her home."

"I'll get some officers together to question the neighbors," Justin offered. "If they had company, maybe someone can get us a description."

"See how far back the footage goes on any security cameras found at any of the neighboring properties," Troy said. "Also, we need to ask the landlord when they moved in. They couldn't have been here more than a few weeks. Randall was on active duty not that long ago."

Justin walked away and started delegating the things Troy had said. Troy didn't pay attention to whom Justin was assigning tasks. That didn't matter. What mattered was the nagging feeling in his gut that everything about this scene was wrong.

He lifted his arm as if holding a gun and aimed it at Ana. Then he looked to where Randall's body was on the floor between the front door and where he stood. The only way someone could have gotten into the house, by Randall, and to the table to shoot Ana straight on was if they had been welcomed into their home.

But that didn't make sense because Randall and Ana couldn't have been in town much longer than Troy had been. He'd only been in town eight days. Who would they have known well enough in eight days that Randall would not only have welcomed them into his home with his new wife but would have let his guard down enough that Ana would have been able to have been murdered in front of him?

It took years to develop that kind of trust. Especially for a guard who was used to seeing the darker side of people. That was why Randall had hidden his marriage to Ana from Troy. The trust was broken there, and he had wanted to protect his wife. He was too smart to let some stranger he didn't know into his home.

Pulling his phone from his pocket, he called the director again. "Did you reach the team?"

"Deon and Powell are on their way in. I haven't been able to reach Hank yet."

Troy's stomach twisted into a tight knot. "When was the last time anyone saw him?"

"I put everyone on leave after we got done questioning them. So...three weeks."

Troy dragged a hand over his face. "Check his phone records. See if he was in contact with Randall during that time."

"That's going to take—"

"Whoever killed Randall and Ana was welcome in their home," he stated. "They weren't expecting what happened to them."

The director was quiet for a moment. "You think it was Hank?"

"I think it was someone who Randall trusted. I think someone convinced Randall I was a monster and used him to frame me. You said Hank is the only member of our team unaccounted for. Who else could get inside Randall's head like that?"

The director let out a loud groan. "Goddamn it," he muttered, but at least he didn't argue with Troy about how Hank would never do something like that. "I'll get on it and call you back as soon as I can."

"Thanks." Troy ended the call and immediately dialed Meri's number. Despite everything he'd seen at the scene, his stress instantly eased at the sound of her voice. When he had said that he'd missed her, he didn't think she could possibly understand how much he'd meant.

"What's going on?" she asked.

"It looks like this was a homicide. I don't have any evidence yet, but I'm starting to suspect Hank was planting some pretty ugly seeds in Randall's head to get him to do the dirty work."

"Oh my God," Meri breathed.

"Are you at the house?"

"Yeah."

"Is Joanie still there?"

"No, she left about fifteen minutes ago."

"Okay. I'm going to wrap things up here and then I'll be on my way." He glanced around before adding, "I love you."

"I love you too," she said, and he could hear the smile in her voice.

Troy ended the call, but he couldn't stop himself from grinning. A day ago, he was worried they'd never recover from all they had gone through. Now he wondered how he had ever doubted that she could understand the mistake he'd made when he had slept with Sarah.

He was about to tell Justin that he wanted copies of Randall's notes once they had been processed when a uniformed officer came rushing into the house.

"We have footage," he called. "We got him!"

[12]

MERI LEANED on the table with her hands wrapped around a cup of coffee as she listened to Logan slowly putting the letters of his new favorite book into words and the words into short sentences.

She had no idea what reading level a six-year-old should be at, but she thought his skills were pretty impressive. She had leaned closer, ready to help him sound out a word that he'd gotten stuck on when she heard a car approaching.

Unlike the other safe house, this one had neighbors, and more times than not, the vehicle drove past them to houses farther down the road. She tilted her head to listen.

This car stopped.

She slid her chair back and walked to the window, expecting to see Troy returning from Randall's.

Her stomach dropped at the sight of Hank Malony easing his car door shut.

"Run!"

And just like that, Logan dashed off.

By the time she pulled her gun and flipped the safety, she heard his bedroom door close. He'd be at the neighbor's house asking them to call 9-1-1 in a matter of minutes. Even so, she held her gun in one hand, ready to fire, and tapped out a text to Troy and Lynn with the other.

9-1-1

They would know that meant trouble. They would come running.

Her heart began painfully pounding in her chest as she watched Hank closing in on the house. The sense of danger she felt was intensified. Not only was the witness she had to protect a sweet, innocent little boy, but she had worked with Hank for a long time. She knew he was good with a gun and with hand-to-hand combat. Everything she knew about his strengths, he also knew about hers.

Though he had to have known better, the first thing he did was try the doorknob. As if she was sitting in a safe house with the door open. What she wasn't expecting, however, was for him to knock and announce his presence.

Did he really expect her to answer?

"Meri," he called through the door. "Meri, it's Hank."

She didn't respond.

He knocked again. "Meri! Open the door!"

"Not a chance you mother...*foxer*," she whispered so he wouldn't hear. She glanced over her shoulder, verifying the bedroom door was secure. She had to delay long enough for Logan to escape.

Two knocks, two pleas to open the door. She had no doubt Hank wasn't going to ask nicely a third time.

As she expected, a loud thud caused the door to shudder. He was kicking at the spot beside the lock. Too bad for him, there were two bolts, and the door was solid oak. She took several deep, calming breaths as he continued kicking. He'd give up soon and shoot at the locks. Then he'd gain entry, and she'd be ready.

Standing off to the side so she didn't get hit by any bullet that might make it through the wood, she stood with her feet shoulder-width apart. Her gun aimed. Her breathing steady. Her finger on the trigger.

He would not get to Logan. He would not hurt that kid.

Four shots was all it took to destroy the bolts. With one more kick, the door flew open, and she was face-to-face with her former teammate. His face was red from his effort, and his breath was loud and choppy. When he caught her gaze, he put his gun on her, but he looked sympathetic about it.

She thought for a moment that it was probably similar to the look she'd given Troy when she'd confronted him.

"I'm not here to hurt you," he said.

"Tell that to the front door," she stated.

"I'm here to protect Logan."

She smirked. "Yeah. I keep hearing that line."

"He's in danger. Troy—"

"Troy was cleared of all charges."

Hank quirked his brow, clearly surprised by what she'd said. "No, Meri. Listen to me. Troy killed the Bantams and took Logan because he needed a ploy to get close to you."

She would have rolled her eyes if she'd dared take them off him for one second.

"Troy has been cleared. Randall set him up."

Hank shook his head. "You can't listen to him. You can't trust him. He has lost his mind."

"He turned himself in. They did an investigation. They released him, Hank. Randall set him up." She saw the confusion in his eyes. He never was very good at having a poker face. "Put your gun down."

He continued with his internal debate before shaking his head, clearly deciding he wasn't going to listen to her. "Where's the boy?"

"Put the gun down," she said again, emphasizing each word.

"He's a Lochlin Private Security asset."

"He's a terrified child. I'm not telling you again. Put the gun down."

Hank kept his weapon on her. "I'm sorry, Meri. But you're no longer a member of our team. You have no right to come between me and my client."

"Hank," she stated, her final warning. "Lower your gun."

"Meri," he said softly in response, "you're standing between me and my job. I don't want to hurt you."

Her finger twitched...

A shot rang out, and Hank took two small steps toward her before falling to his knees and crumpling onto the floor at her feet.

The shot had come from behind him.

She looked at the door, expecting to see Troy or one of the Prestige team members. Instead, Director Bruce stepped through, his gun still aimed at Hank. Meri finally exhaled the breath she'd barely been allowing so she could hold her gun steady. Lowering her weapon, she let out a slight laugh as relief filled her.

"Holy shit," she whispered. "I thought you were in New York."

"I flew back with Troy. He didn't tell you?"

She shook her head. "No." She watched him take Hank's pulse before she felt safe enough to holster her weapon. "Where is he?"

"He's still at Randall's." The director stood and smiled. "It's just us. You and me. And *Logan*."

Meri creased her brow. His tone, his posture, the strange look in his eyes. The hair on the nape of her neck stood as her instinct screamed at her that she was still in danger. Lowering her gaze to his right hand, she noticed he was still holding a weapon. But it wasn't his. He'd taken the gun from Hank's hand. He had his finger on the trigger. If he had to shoot someone—her...*Logan*—he was going to use Hank's weapon.

"Where is he?"

She stood a bit taller, more aware, but didn't want to let him know she'd realized something was off. Instead of telling him the kid had long ago climbed from the window and was seeking help, she licked her lip and nodded down the hall. "He's hiding. Let me go get him," she said. "Tell him it's safe."

She stared him down but didn't open her mouth.

"Tell him to come out, Meri."

After swallowing hard, she managed to shake her head.

"He won't come out unless I use our secret code. I have to knock out a pattern."

He tilted his head. "Meri. Tell him to come out. Right now."

Any doubt that she might have had vanished. Suddenly it all made sense. The killer was someone on the inside who could plant evidence and turn the other guards against Troy. Someone on the inside could find and murder the Bantams without being caught. Someone who had hidden the payoff so well that it couldn't be traced.

Or someone so high on the food chain that his accounts hadn't been investigated.

He smiled a know-it-all smile. He realized she'd finally figured him out.

"Logan!" he yelled.

The house remained silent. The bedroom door stayed closed.

"He won't come out," she told him.

He didn't listen. "Logan. If you don't come out right now, I'm going to shoot Meri. I'm going to kill her."

"You idiot," she said with a smirk. "He's long gone. We didn't show him where to hide. We showed him how to escape. He's gone."

"You're lying."

She shook her head at him. "How could you do this? How much did they pay you to sell your soul?"

He smiled. "Sell my soul?"

"You killed them for money, and now you're trying to wrap up your messy-ass job by killing Logan. Why?"

"Why does anyone do anything, Meri? I needed the

money. Bantam was dirty. He was laundering money through his company and got greedy. Pissed off the wrong people."

"And you sold him out. You were supposed to be protecting him. His son! You're going to kill a kid for money?"

"No. I was only going to kill Richard. Troy and his damn gut feelings. If he hadn't taken them to a safe house, Sharon and Logan never would have gotten caught up in this. I could have killed Richard, and they could have gone on with their lives. Troy did this."

"Seriously?" Meri asked. "You're blaming Troy for being too good at his job? That's your excuse for hunting down a little boy?"

The director lifted his gun, taking aim at her head. "I didn't want to hurt him, but I won't lose everything over a kid. Or a former employee."

Meri swallowed. The cold look in his eyes made it clear that she was out of time. She slid to the left as she reached for her gun in one quick movement. She had just grasped the butt when the director pulled his trigger.

Pain burned her right arm as the bullet grazed her. She was still able to pull her Glock from her hip. However, before she could take aim, she heard the distinct sound of Logan screaming.

As she looked over her shoulder, he opened his bedroom door and ran toward her.

"No!" she ordered, but he kept running anyway. Putting her body between the director and Logan, she gasped as another bullet hit her. This time above her right hip. If she hadn't blocked the way, Logan would have taken the shot. That knowledge gave her the strength to ignore the pain and finish what had been started.

She managed to get two shots off. She didn't know where they hit Director Bruce, but he jerked twice before stumbling back.

Grabbing Logan's hand, she dragged him toward the door. She had to get him out of the house. Stumbling across the deck, she managed to get them to the stairs before a car came speeding down the road.

Troy.

Meri focused on getting Logan down the stairs and into Troy's arms. That was all that mattered. Troy could save him. She had to save him. She made it to the stairs before her strength started to fade.

"Go," she said, urging Logan to run faster. "Get to Troy."

"Meri!" a voice called from behind her.

She spun as Director Bruce stopped on the deck, glaring at her. Raising her gun, she got off two more shots. One missed, but the other hit him in the forehead. She watched him collapse on the wood before she fell to her knees, no longer able to stand.

The pain was too much, and her head was spinning.

But Logan was safe.

That was all that mattered, she told herself as she closed her eyes and fell forward.

Relief rushed through Troy as he carried Logan into the room where Meri was after a surgeon removed the bullet from her hip and stitched her up. Her face was pale, but she opened her eyes and offered them a soft smile.

Logan squirmed down and rushed to the bed.

"Take it easy, bud," Troy warned.

"It's okay," Meri said weakly as she lifted her arms. Logan climbed onto the bed and gave her a hug. "Oh, you scared me," she said, hugging him close.

"You scared me too," he said. "You got shot."

Troy ruffled his hair. "She's okay."

"I'm better than okay," Meri said. "How are you?"

Logan sank back. "I'm okay. I'm sorry I didn't listen. I was scared to leave you with the bad guy."

"It's okay," Meri told him. "I'm glad you didn't get hurt."

"But you did," Logan said quietly.

"I'm all right."

Troy couldn't be happier about that. She had lost some blood, but she would be fine. He had a million questions about what had happened, but that was going to have to wait.

Lynn said the police who were investigating were already starting to figure some things out. As soon as Troy had seen the director approach Randall's house on the security footage, everything fell into place. Well, not everything, but enough for him to realize his entire team had been patsies for the director's scheme—whatever his scheme had been.

They hadn't found money in the man's accounts like Troy had expected they would, but they'd found the files on

Meri. The director had known all along that Troy wasn't behind the images. He'd set him up and turned his team against him.

When Troy had pressed Deon and Powell about what had happened that night, they confirmed the director had called and ordered them outside to check the perimeter. When they returned, the Bantams were dead. There was no evidence that the director himself killed the couple, but he had made it possible for someone else to. Until they found out who, there could still be danger, but for the most part, Troy felt comfortable that the mole had been found, and as soon as Logan was placed in a new safe house, he'd be safe.

Lochlin Private Security was going to put him with someone. A family member, but if one couldn't be found, the boy would end up in foster care.

Tears unexpectedly stung Troy's tears. A side effect of being so damn exhausted, he decided as he blinked before Meri could notice. But she looked up at him, and her eyes were also glazed. He knew her heart was aching too. She knew the score.

"Oh my God," Trista said as her eyes grew wide. "You guys are so much cuter than the Donnellys ever were."

Troy laughed softly as he sat back. However, when he looked at her, he realized that Trista hadn't come in to tell them that they were adorable.

"What is it?"

Her face sagged, and sadness touched her eyes. "There are some guards here to transport Logan."

Damn it. That was sooner than Troy was expecting.

Meri hugged Logan closer and pressed her nose into his curls.

"No," Logan whined and tightened his hold on Meri.

"It's okay," she whispered. She kissed his head, but the dread in her eyes as she looked at Troy was unmistakable. She didn't want to let him go. "Listen, buddy, they're going to take care of you now."

"I want to stay with you."

"I know," she said. "I wish I could take care of you forever, but I can't."

"But you're my mom now. We said so."

Meri closed her eyes and creased her brow. "Troy will be with you. He's going to stay with you."

"What about you?"

She looked up at Troy. Asking her to explain that she'd never be allowed to see him again was a bit much given all she'd been through. Troy reached down and tugged Logan's hold on her free and lifted him off the bed.

"We'll talk to Meri soon, okay?" Troy said.

"Go," Meri said.

Troy hesitated. Opened his mouth. This was goodbye. And he didn't know how long it would be before he would see her again. They had to sort through all the evidence, come to a conclusion, make sure there was no more threat to Logan. And then, Troy could come back. But he didn't know how long that would be.

"Logan comes first," she said as if she could read his mind. "Always. Go."

Leaning down, he put a kiss on her lips and whispered, "I'm coming back for you."

She smiled as she touched his cheek. "You better. And for the love of God, would you please shave first?"

Troy laughed softly. "I'll consider it."

Her smile softened. "I'll see you."

"See you."

Focusing on Logan, she gave him that same fake reassuring smile she had the day that they had barged into her life. "Take care of Troy for me, okay?"

He hugged Troy tight and nodded. "Bye, Meri," he said weakly.

"Bye, Logan."

"Here we go, buddy," Troy said as he hefted Logan up. "Take care of her," he whispered to Lynn, though he knew he didn't have to. Her team would be there for her. They'd take care of her.

He didn't put Logan down again until they were rushing into a car waiting for them. Once inside, they were whisked off toward the airport. Everything was a blur—getting tickets, boarding a flight, taking off. His mind didn't stop spinning until they were high in the air, leaving Meri far behind them.

Logan stared at the book in his hands, but he didn't open it or flip the pages. Once again, Troy was tearing this kid's world apart with the intention of keeping him safe.

Dragging a hand over his face, he played the day over again in his mind. He wanted to laugh at how much they had been through in less than twenty-four hours, but he couldn't. It was too much. It was all too much.

"Troy?"

Blinking his dry eyes, he looked at Logan. "Yeah?"

He lifted his little face, and Troy noticed the tears that had soaked his cheeks. "Is Meri mad at me?"

"No, of course not. She's so happy that nothing bad happened to you."

"I heard the bad guy. I didn't want him to hurt her like he hurt my mom and dad."

Troy sat back. "That was the same bad guy? The one who came to your house?"

Logan nodded. "I peeked out of my door when I heard noises. I know I wasn't supposed to—"

"It's okay," Troy said. "And you saw the same man there that hurt Meri?"

Logan nodded. "I didn't want him to hurt Meri, so I didn't leave like she'd told me. He hurt her anyway."

"She's going to be okay," Troy said.

Logan's lip trembled. "Then why did we leave her?"

"We had to, Logan. She's going to be okay. Lynn and Joanie and all the Prestige team are there to take care of her."

He looked at his book again. "But she's my mom now," he said. "We shouldn't have left her."

Troy didn't have a clue how he was supposed to respond to that. How much damage could he do to one kid? Looking out the window at the darkness below them, Troy ruffled Logan's hair and tugged him into as much of a hug as he could give him in the airplane seat.

He wouldn't press Logan for more now, the boy had been through enough, but once they were rested, he intended to do everything he could to confirm Ron Bruce had killed the Bantams and that there was no further risk to Logan.

Once he no longer needed to be protected by Lochlin Private Security, they were going to have to find a home for him. Troy was already working on solving that problem too. He was going to do everything in his power to make sure Logan didn't ever have to leave his side again.

EPILOGUE

Three months later...

Meri's mind faded as the morning meeting started. The members of Prestige were a chatty bunch, and she usually took it upon herself to get them to focus, but she was the one with the wandering mind these days.

She hadn't talked to Tory since they'd gotten back to New York. He'd called to let her know that they were putting Logan and him into another safe house until they knew for certain no one else was after the kid.

That had been three months ago.

Meri glanced at her phone. She knew he couldn't call, but that didn't stop her from checking. She imagined, wherever they were and whatever they were doing, Logan was stuck to Troy like glue. She never would have thought that she'd miss having someone trailing her every move, but she had gotten so used to having Logan a step behind her that she'd been quite lonely without him.

When he'd first met her, he didn't have much to say. But

by the time he'd left, he'd barely stopped talking. She hoped that they had found time to look for rocks. He had been so excited to do that. Though Troy wouldn't have the same knowledge as Shawn, she thought they would probably enjoy looking up the information together.

He hadn't been able to take his books with him, though. Meri had specifically asked Joanie to buy him books on rocks and space. He'd had to leave those behind. She still had them. Maybe someday she could send them to him. She doubted Lochlin Private Security would allow it, but she could hope that her history with the agency would be taken into consideration and they'd forward the package to him.

"Hey, are you okay?" Marta asked, gently nudging Meri.

Meri considered lying, but that would be pointless. Her teammate would see through her. "They were only here a week. I shouldn't be so attached."

"A week of high stress and a lot of emotion," Joanie offered. "It's okay that you got attached to them."

"I've never been much for kids," Meri said. "But that little guy was..."

"He was awesome," Marta said. "And Troy?" She fanned herself and chuckled.

Meri laughed too. "Yeah." After giving her head a hard shake, she cleared her throat.

Lynn walked into the conference room. "Do you have a way to reach out to him?"

"No. They're in hiding until they can confirm Logan is safe."

"I'm sorry."

Meri shook her head. "It's fine. I'm fine. I'll take the rest of the day off to clear my head."

"Take all the time you need," Lynn said. "Oh, and since you are leaving, before I got to this point on the agenda, Lochlin is reimbursing Prestige for all expenses related to protecting Logan and then some. We're not taking a loss for that."

"I'm really glad to hear that."

Lynn smiled. "Yeah, me too. I was kind of shitting my pants trying to figure how we were going to bounce back from that."

"I know you were. Thank you for not letting that stop you from looking after him."

"Go home," Lynn said.

As Meri drove home, she tried to determine how long she was going to wait for Troy before getting herself out of this depressive rut she had let herself slip into.

There had been times when agents were on a case for months or even longer. She had no idea how long it would be before he could resurface, and until then, she was on her own. Maybe she should move.

She really missed that little house on the pond where they had first stayed. They hadn't even had a chance to settle in, but she had loved the house. She should check to see if it was still available to rent.

It was a bit high for her budget, but she could make it work. And it would be worth it to be able to sit on the deck, sipping coffee, as she looked out over the pond. Though she probably should move someplace that didn't have ghosts of Troy and Logan haunting it.

Meri slowed as she neared her driveway, where a black sedan sat. The sticker in the back window indicated it was a rental, which confused her even more.

Parking next to the unfamiliar vehicle, she checked her weapon and climbed out of the car. She wasn't expecting trouble, but she wasn't going to face whoever had invaded her driveway unprepared.

She cautiously approached her house when she heard voices inside. Whoever was there wasn't hiding. Turning the knob, she found her front door unlocked. Easing the door open, she peered inside and was immediately hit with scents she hadn't smelled in over a year.

Her mom's homemade meatballs.

Barely inside her living room, she stopped and stared. Not only was her mom there, stirring sauce on her stove, but Troy was sitting at the island. He'd brought her mother to visit.

Meri's heart more than lifted. It all but took flight. She was about to ask what they were doing there when she was startled by a flash of movement.

"Meri!" Logan screamed as he ran across the room.

Stunned, she only found the strength to move when he reached her. Scooping him up, she hugged the little guy that she was certain she'd never see again.

"Meri," he grunted. "Your hug is too tight."

Chuckling, she eased her hold on him. "What are you doing here?"

"I get to live with Troy now. The judge said so. He's really, *really* my dad now, and you get to really, *really* be my mom. Isn't that awesome?"

She lifted her brows and opened her mouth, but no words formed.

Troy put his hand on Logan's head. "Go taste the sauce, huh?" As soon as Logan darted off, he put his hand on her head. "Hi."

She laughed. "Hi."

"How are you?"

Meri bit her lips, imagining that her smile was as big and goofy as a schoolgirl with a crush. "Uh. Shocked. How are you?"

"Pretty amazing, actually."

"You're his guardian?"

Troy nodded. "There are some hoops to jump through and all that, but we're working on making it permanent."

"You're adopting him?"

He shrugged. "He grew on me." A slight bit of insecurity that she wasn't expecting touched his eyes. "I'm hoping he grew on you too. Looks like we're a package deal."

"Well," she said, rolling her head back as if thinking. "I guess if I want Logan around, I can put up with you too."

"Hey," he playfully chastised. Putting his hands on her hips, he pulled her to him. "Oh. I didn't hurt you, did I?"

"No. I'm fine." Wrapping her arms around his neck, she put her forehead to his. "I'm very happy you're a package deal. I've missed you guys."

"Yeah?"

She nodded.

"That's good. I was hoping you'd say that. There's a reason I brought your mom with me."

Meri grinned. "Besides her meatballs."

"My attorney says that the adoption would be easier if..."

She widened her eyes. "If?"

"We were going to get married sometime anyway. Why not now?"

Well, she wasn't expecting that. "Now?" Meri took a step back. "Like...*now*?"

"Now, Meri," her mother called. "For God's sake, you two have been playing googly eyes for years."

She gawked at the woman standing in her kitchen. "Ma!"

The little woman pulled Logan with her from the kitchen. "Go get the thing," she ordered, and he ran off. "The boy needs parents and a home," her mom said, coming into the living room. "He needs a nice grandmother to put some weight on him. He's too thin."

"Oh boy," Meri muttered, but she wasn't irritated. She couldn't possibly be irritated. She was so happy to see them all again. She put a kiss on her mother's cheek. "Leave him alone. He's fine."

"He needs more pasta in his diet."

Meri chuckled. "Have you seen him scarf down a bowl of mac and cheese?"

"Got it," Logan said, running back to them. Grinning, he held up a box for Troy.

A gasp left Meri's lips. She knew that box. She'd seen it a million times at her mother's house. Her grandmother's wedding ring was inside that box.

"Troy? You're serious?"

He opened the box and grinned as he eased to one knee. Slipping his arm around Logan, he pulled the boy close.

"Marry us?"

Laughing, she held her hand out and let him slip the ring on her finger.

"Yes!" Logan said with a fist pump.

"It's about time," her mother muttered and went back to the kitchen to check her food. Logan was right behind her, asking if he could try the sauce again.

"You didn't invite her to live with us, did you?" Meri asked as Troy stood.

"Oh, hell no." Hugging her against him, he laughed slightly. "Are you really okay with this? We kind of bombarded you."

"As you tend to do." Sliding her hands up his arms, she wrapped her arms around his neck. She watched Logan laugh as her mother teased him before letting him have a spoon. "I'm okay with this."

"I'm glad, because there's one more thing. I know how much you love your job and, frankly, I've kind of had enough of mine. I quit so we could move here. The judge did approve this, before you ask, but I'm slightly unemployed at the moment."

Meri gawked at him. "Slightly?"

"*Completely*. However, I have a few ideas. I know someone who works at a security firm, and I thought maybe, if you were okay with it, I'd apply."

"I think I'd be okay with that." Leaning up, she kissed him softly. "I think I'd be more than okay with that."

ALSO BY MARCI BOLDEN

STONEHILL SERIES:

The Road Leads Back

Friends Without Benefits

The Forgotten Path

Jessica's Wish

This Old Café

Forever Yours

THE WOMEN OF HEARTS SERIES:

Hidden Hearts

Burning Hearts

Stolen Hearts

Secret Hearts

Cheating Hearts

Runaway Hearts

OTHER TITLES:

California Can Wait

Seducing Kate

A Life Without Water

ABOUT THE AUTHOR

As a teen, Marci Bolden skipped over young adult books and jumped right into reading romance novels. She never left.

Marci lives in the Midwest with her husband, kiddos, and numerous rescue pets. If she had an ounce of willpower, Marci would embrace healthy living, but until cupcakes and wine are no longer available at the local market, she will appease her guilt by reading self-help books and promising to join a gym "soon."

Visit her here:
www.marcibolden.com

facebook.com/MarciBoldenAuthor
x.com/BoldenMarci
instagram.com/marciboldenauthor

Milton Keynes UK
Ingram Content Group UK Ltd.
UKHW020932220724
445981UK00001B/40